SOCCER DUEL

Terry could not _____ ng. The unpleasant fact was that he, Terry Masters, was outside the spotlight. The glare of stardom was on Krystian Wisniewski. Nobody was cheering Terry Masters, and he could not help noticing. Sure, he had been in other games when a teammate's outstanding play won the loudest cheers. But always before Terry knew that he had had the cheers and he would have them again. He was a star. He knew it. Until now.

"Say," Terry's father said when they were in the car, "that Polish boy—what's his name?—is one whale of a player, isn't he?"

"Dygard has combined the soccer upsurge, the superiority of experienced foreigners, and the dethronement of an American standout to produce an unusual story with his usual strong fictional values."
—Kirkus Reviews

Soccer Duel

Thomas J. Dygard

Puffin Books

PUFFIN BOOKS
Published by the Penguin Group
Viking Penguin, a division of Penguin Books USA Inc.,
40 West 23rd Street, New York, New York 10010, U.S.A.
Penguin Books Ltd, 27 Wrights Lane, London W8 5TZ, England
Penguin Books Australia Ltd, Ringwood, Victoria, Australia
Penguin Books Canada Ltd, 2801 John Street, Markham, Ontario, Canada L3R 1B4
Penguin Books (N.Z.) Ltd, 182–190 Wairau Road, Auckland 10, New Zealand

Penguin Books Ltd, Registered Offices: Harmondsworth, Middlesex, England

First published in the United States of America by William Morrow and Company, Inc., 1981
Reprinted by arrangement with William Morrow and Company, Inc.
Published in Puffin Books, 1990
1 3 5 7 9 10 8 6 4 2
Copyright © Thomas J. Dygard, 1981
All rights reserved

LIBRARY OF CONGRESS CATALOGING IN PUBLICATION DATA
Dygard, Thomas J.   Soccer duel / Thomas J. Dygard.   p.   cm.
Reprint. Originally published: New York : Morrow, 1981.
Summary: A former football star finds he must share the spotlight
with other players when he decides to play soccer.
ISBN 0-14-034116-1
[1. Soccer—Fiction.]   I. Title.
PZ7.D9893So 1990   [Fic]—dc20   89-10602

Printed in the United States of America
by Arcata Graphics, Kingsport, Tennessee
Set in Times Roman

Dedicated to Coach Steve Dezurko
and his Arlington High Cardinals,
soccer team of Arlington Heights, Illinois,
with admiration and appreciation.

Soccer Duel

Chapter 1

Now that the day had finally arrived, Terry Masters awoke with an uneasy feeling.

He swung his feet to the floor and sat for a moment on the side of the bed, rubbing the sleep out of his eyes. The late-summer sun was streaming through the window. The rays angled through the glass walls of a terrarium near the head of the bed, producing a faint rainbow. Inside the terrarium an iguana pawed listlessly at the glass.

"Good morning, Fred," Terry said to the iguana.

The walls of the room were covered with the memorabilia

11

of two years at Windsor High School. A maroon pennant with *Windsor Eagles* emblazoned on it in white letters hung on the wall opposite the bed. Below the pennant were three group pictures, each in its own black frame: the football team, the basketball team, the baseball team. Alongside the row of group pictures, another frame held a picture of a football player in action: number 32 carrying the ball and deftly eluding a tackler.

Against another wall stood a bookcase. The shelves were packed with books. Most of them were sports books: biographies of sports heroes, novels about football, baseball, and basketball, a few technical sports books bearing the names of famous coaches.

Atop the bookcase, carefully centered and standing alone, was a small trophy. The golden figure of a football player, with the ball tucked safely away in the right hand, was poised with the left hand extended to fend off a tackler. The brass plate on the mahogany base of the trophy was inscribed: "Terry Masters, Most Valuable Player, Freshman Team, Windsor High School."

Terry glanced at the trophy.

He had come close to winning the varsity trophy in his sophomore season last year. The bitter disappointment still flickered whenever his eyes caught the freshman trophy. He should have had the varsity trophy to stand alongside it on the bookcase. He had scored eleven touchdowns from his halfback position and finished the season being the team's

12

leading ground gainer. He had been, indisputably, the star of the Windsor High Eagles football team. The chatter among the players was that Terry was a cinch to win the trophy, the first sophomore in Windsor High's history to do so. However, the coaches voted the trophy to a senior lineman, the team's leading tackler. Terry understood what had happened. For the senior lineman, it was the last chance. For Terry, there were two more chances. In a close vote, the senior was bound to get the edge. But Terry was still deeply disappointed.

He stood up and stretched his arms above his head and yawned.

In his sleeping shorts, Terry Masters stood an even six feet tall and weighed one hundred and eighty pounds. He had broad shoulders and muscular arms. His stomach was flat and appeared hard as a board. He had narrow hips and thick, sturdy thighs. His was the perfect body of a three-sport athlete—football, basketball, baseball.

His dark brown hair, straight and long—too long, his father always said—flopped down around his ears as he ran a hand through it.

The frown creasing his forehead was evident when he shoved the hair aside. The frown had been there when he awoke. Today, Terry knew, was going to be tough, very tough. He would be glad when it was over.

"Terry, are you up?" his mother called from the foot of the stairs.

"Yes, I'm up," he said.

"You're scheduled for the nine o'clock group for school registration, you know."

"Yes, I know." His voice carried a touch of irritation.

"Are you all right?"

"I'm fine," Terry said, trying to keep the irritable tone out of his answer. He was always amazed at his mother's ability to detect and interpret the slightest inflection in his voice.

School registration at nine o'clock meant getting his classroom schedule, finding out which teachers he had drawn, having his picture taken for the yearbook, checking out textbooks, and buying notebooks for the coming semester. It meant, too, seeing friends from the year before and meeting some of the new arrivals at Windsor High. There were sure to be plenty of new people. There always were. In Windsor, a suburb of Chicago, families moved in and out quickly, following the father's career. A lifelong resident of Windsor like Terry Masters was a rarity.

School registration also meant sign-up time—for the staff of the school newspaper, the yearbook staff, the debating team, the chess club, the sports teams, and the myriad of other extracurricular activities. Each one had a table in the gymnasium, manned by a faculty sponsor and a student, with a clipboard holding a sign-up list. Students milled around in the gymnasium, made their decisions, walked up to the table of their choice, and signed their names.

14

"And that is when it will hit the fan," Terry mumbled to himself, as he went down the short hallway to the bathroom for his morning shower.

Terry Masters was going to walk past the table for football sign-up to the table where the boys were signing up for the soccer team. He was going to sign himself up for the soccer team. He was not going to play football. A boy could play only one or the other, because the seasons ran parallel. And Terry had decided on soccer.

Terry stepped into the shower and came awake, really awake, when the needles of hot water hit his body.

He wondered, as he had before, when exactly he had made the decision for soccer instead of football. Surely there was an instant, a single moment, when his brain said: soccer, not football. He knew only that in two years of playing park-district soccer in the summer he had come to love the game. He loved it too much to give it up. And one day he just realized that he was not going to give it up. He was going to play soccer instead of football.

Until today the decision had been Terry's closely held secret.

Not even Hank Dodsworth knew of his intention. Hank, Terry's best friend and a teammate in baseball, was the one who talked Terry into giving soccer a try in the first place. Hank, the goalie on the Eagles soccer team, had played grade-school soccer in St. Louis before moving to Windsor with his family. He had grown up playing soccer. "It's a beautiful game," he kept telling Terry. "If you learn to play soccer, you'll forget about football." Terry finally bowed to his friend's urging. With the end of the high-school baseball season in the spring, he had joined Hank's team in the summertime park-district league. That was two summers ago. From the start, Terry was hooked on the game. His natural athletic ability enabled him to pick up the skills in short order. He quickly agreed with Hank: "It's a beautiful game." But at the end of that first summer he left soccer when football practice started. He never considered anything else. Then, this past summer, with his skills sharpening on the soccer field, Terry made the decision—when?—to go out for soccer instead of football at Windsor High.

Hank had seemed to sense Terry's thoughts as the season drew to a close and the play ended in the park-district league. "You're going to do it," Hank gibed. "You're going to play for the Eagles soccer team this fall instead of the football team."

"Ah, go away," Terry answered, grinning.

The decision hadn't been an easy one for Terry to live with, once he'd made it. He had been a major factor in the Windsor High football team's record of seven victories and two losses last season. Fast and strong, he was blessed with an instinctive—almost spooky—ability to determine where holes in the line were going to open up. He was surely a big part of Coach Wilson Brundage's plans for an even better record in the coming season.

Terry shuddered at the thought of the football coach's reaction to his decision to drop football. Brundage was going to hit the ceiling. When it came to temper, Wilson Brundage had no match. When Brundage blew his stack, the trees shook for blocks around. Terry dreaded the interview with the football coach.

His teammates, too, would be—what?—angry and puzzled and bitter and disappointed. Wilson Brundage was not the only one relying on Terry Masters's football talents for the coming season. Terry recalled Steve Palmer, the quarterback and team captain, talking during the summer about the chances for an undefeated season. For the first time in years, every key player seemed sure to return to the team for another season. Not a one had moved away from Windsor during the off-season. Was Steve Palmer going to feel that Terry had betrayed them? Were the others?

There was Terry's father, too. Stepping out of the shower and reaching for a towel, Terry moaned almost audibly at the thought of his father's reaction.

Alvin Masters had been an All-American halfback at Maryland. Alvin Masters had encouraged, nurtured, and gloried in his son's football successes. The night that Terry was born, according to the family story, Alvin Masters appeared at the hospital with a football for his son. Knowing his father, Terry was not sure that the story was just a funny line. It probably had happened that way. Terry's mother confirmed that Alvin Masters's first comment upon viewing his new son had been, "He's built like a runner." Terry was sure Alvin Masters was not going to be pleased at his son's decision to abandon football for soccer. For Alvin Masters, the decision would mean a dream vanishing in a puff of smoke: another Masters on the All-American football teams. Disappointing his father would not be pleasant for Terry.

But Terry had made his decision. For him, it was the right one. He was sure of it.

He finished drying and, with the towel wrapped around his waist, walked back down the hallway to his bedroom.

He wondered again when the actual moment of decision had occurred. At what instant did he know? His mind worked back to a day in mid-July, about a week after the Fourth, when he was playing a match. His team, the Rockets, and the Torpedoes were locked in a scoreless duel for the park-district league lead. Time was running out. Terry got the ball just on the forward side of the halfway line, near the touchline at the edge of the playing area. He began dribbling toward an opening. He maneuvered the ball well with his feet. Terry was right-footed and still favored the use of his right foot. The weakness was natural for a player in only his second year of soccer. Terry had not grown up dribbling a soccer ball, developing equal dexterity with each of his feet. But the weeks of hard work during the two summers of soccer were paying off, and Terry dribbled with surprising ability and confidence.

With his speed and agility, he eluded one defender and

found himself facing Bones Nelson, the best player on the Windsor Eagles soccer team last season. Bones Nelson, quick and skilled, was a formidable defender. Terry made a shoulder fake to the left. Bones took the bait. He leaned with the fake. Terry nudged the ball the other way, to his right. Then he circled the off-balance Bones and picked up the dribble. He could not help smiling as he left the confused Bones behind. Bones uttered a funny little exclamation—"Oh!"—acknowledging that he had been outsmarted and outplayed. By that time, Terry was headed for the goal.

At ten yards out, with defenders converging on him, Terry kicked the ball with the outside of his left foot, sending a pass to a teammate. Terry continued his run toward the goal, looking for open space. The teammate, with the goalie moving over to cover him, kicked a grass burner of a pass back to Terry. Terry, on the run, sidestepped a full-back, planted his left foot, and swung his right foot through. Too late, the goalie turned his attention back to Terry and tried to recover. Terry's kick sent the ball soaring past the goalie's frantic leap and into the nets, winning the match. Bones Nelson, seconds too late, flashed by Terry as the ball hit the nets.

The whole play—from the moment of possession near the halfway line, through the victorious dribble, the instant of the pass and the return pass, the impact of his foot on the ball, kicking for goal—added up to the biggest thrill Terry ever had experienced in sports.

He loved the game, and he knew it.

He knew something else, too. He had whipped the best of the Windsor High Eagles soccer players, Bones Nelson, in a duel in the open field. He could play with the best of them on the Windsor High varsity. He could beat the best of them. He had just done it.

Yes, Terry thought, as he buckled his jeans, pulled on a T-shirt, and headed downstairs, that must have been the moment when he knew he would go out for soccer, not football.

The memory of the play had wiped the frown off Terry's face by the time he sat down to breakfast at the kitchen table.

Chapter 2

Terry spotted Horst Schmidt, the soccer coach of the Windsor High Eagles, seated at a table on the opposite side of the gymnasium.

The gym was buzzing with activity. Tables were lined up around all four walls. A large white card with black lettering announced the extracurricular activity each table represented. The tables for the three fall sports—football, cross-country track, and soccer—were in a row.

The center of the gymnasium floor was crowded. Students milled from one table to another, chattering with each other, renewing the friendships from last year, meeting new students.

The start of classes was still two weeks away. But for the students, the registration day marked the end of the summer vacation and the start of the new school year. Windsor High was back in action, the center of life for the more than twelve hundred students.

Terry had completed the ritual of registration in the school cafeteria, next to the gym. He had stood in the long line to get his classroom schedule. He had checked out his textbooks and bought his notebooks. He had donned the dress shirt, necktie, and navy-blue jacket provided by the photographer in a variety of sizes and had his picture taken for the yearbook.

Now, entering the gym, Terry felt again the uneasiness, the discomfort. His frown was back in place.

Terry glanced from Horst Schmidt to the football table. More than a dozen boys were standing in front of it, waiting their turns at the clipboard to sign up for the football team. None of the boys noticed Terry across the crowded gymnasium floor. They were intent on getting their turn at the clipboard. As Terry made his way across the room he saw that Wilson Brundage was nowhere in sight. A pair of student managers were handling the sign-up procedure. Terry was relieved. There would be time later to tell Brundage about his decision. Terry wanted Brundage to hear of the decision from him and not through the chatter of the students as the word spread. But he didn't want to tell Brundage at the football table, in front of the gawking crowd of football teammates.

He moved toward the soccer table.

"Good morning, Terry," Schmidt said. The greeting, spoken with a heavy German accent, came out sounding like *Guten Morgen.*

Terry knew the history of Horst Schmidt. He had been a world-class soccer player in Germany before he was out of his teens. But the siren call of the North American Soccer League's money in the infant days of the league lured him to the United States. He was one of many sparkling foreign players imported into the United States to give the fledgling league a lineup of professionals in a country that had produced precious few of its own. The sport was just getting started in the United States. Schmidt played three years for the Chicago Sting and was a glittering ornament of the league. Then, one night against the Dallas Tornadoes, he was injured in a freak tangle of arms and legs and carried from the field. The limp was hardly noticeable now, but Horst Schmidt would never play world-class soccer again.

However, Horst Schmidt had more than the quick feet, the balance, the stamina, the power, and the skill of a top soccer player. He had brains, too. He had attended universities in Europe, and in his three years as a professional soccer player in the United States he had attended college in the off-season and taken correspondence courses during the season. In three years he completed his education, winning a master's degree in education. So when he left the hospital and then laid down the crutches, he became a German teacher at Windsor High in the suburbs of the city where he had starred. He was teaching German on that day, three years before, when the School Board decided to recognize the growing interest in soccer and add the sport to the varsity list at Windsor High. Who would coach the new Windsor Eagles soccer team? Who else?

Terry knew Horst Schmidt from the classroom, too. Schmidt had quickly gained a reputation as tough teacher—demanding, heavy on the homework, a "low grader" who was stingy with the A's and merciless when it came to dealing out the F's. From Terry's own experience in first-year German the year before, he could testify that the corridor gossip about Horst Schmidt was accurate. Terry got out with a grade of B in both semesters, although he would have sailed home with an easy A in any other course that he worked so hard in. He suspected there were no A's at all. Nobody seemed to satisfy Horst Schmidt sufficiently to warrant an excellent rating. But Terry liked him. He had to admit that the German teacher inspired him, or drove him, or hectored him into giving the course his best.

"Good morning, Coach," Terry said, returning Schmidt's smile.

Despite the years of inactivity since his injury, Horst Schmidt looked fit. He had done nothing more athletic than

24

show a player how to put a foot into the ball to get the spin
—and the arc—desired. But unmistakably, here was an
athlete. Schmidt was not large, probably not quite six feet
tall. He was slender, in the sort of packed-in way that Terry
had noticed in a lot of athletes, and looked as if he weighed
a hundred and fifty pounds. More likely, he probably
weighed about a hundred and sixty—no fat, just bone and
muscle with a tight covering of skin. Schmidt somehow
conveyed the image of movement—quick, flitting movement—even when sitting perfectly still. He wore his black
hair cropped short, combed to the side. His face, with its
strong jaw and thin, beaked nose, was one everyone had
seen in the newspapers and magazines when the great German soccer star was in his prime.

"You had a good summer with park-district soccer,"
Schmidt said. Schmidt had coached one of the teams that
Terry's Rockets competed against. The coach spoke in easy
conversation, making no move to pass across the clipboard
on which a prospective soccer player might sign up. "You
made me wish you were on my soccer team."

"Thanks," Terry said. "Instead, I want to be on your team
this fall."

Schmidt's thick, black eyebrows shot up. "Eh?" he said.

"I've decided that I want to play soccer this year instead
of football."

Schmidt said nothing for a moment. He seemed to be
enjoying a fleeting private thought. Then he said, "That's

wonderful, Terry. We will be glad to have you on the team. The Eagles can use your abilities."

Schmidt turned the clipboard around for Terry to sign.

Yes, Terry thought, the Eagles can use me. As in most schools in the suburbs, virtually all of Windsor High's superior athletes signed up for football. Football was the traditional autumn game for the outstanding athlete. That was where the crowds were. That was where the cheers were. That was where the glory of playing was. Except for the few foreign students, soccer had no place in the background of most of the students attending Windsor High. The athletes had been raised on football, and they played it if they could. What was left for the soccer team, for the most part, were those less gifted and too small for football, plus the occasional foreign student who chanced to enroll. The Eagles, in their second year of the soccer program, had posted a disappointing 10-8-1 record, and they lost out in the first round of the district tournament, leading to the state championship. Yes, Terry told himself, the Eagles can use me. He had seen himself on the field against the area's soccer players—Americans and foreigners alike— and he knew he met the measure of all of them.

Terry scanned the page on the clipboard.

The first name on the list was Hank Dodsworth. Terry smiled at the sight of the name. Hank, being in the eight o'clock registration group, had signed when the page was blank. He had long since left the school building for home, not knowing Terry would be here signing up. Terry resolved to call Hank with the word when he got home.

There was Harold Nelson's name. For a moment Terry was puzzled. Then he identified Bones Nelson. He had not known that Bones' real name was Harold. Terry's mind flashed back to that game in July, and he relived the exhilaration of faking Bones out of position, circling around him, and then driving for the goal that won the match. Bones, heading into his senior year at Windsor High, was the established star of the Eagles soccer team. But he had lost to Terry that day. Bones Nelson can get ready to move over, Terry thought.

The other names, too, were familiar to Terry. There was Henrik Sterner, the jolly madman of the moped. Only this morning Terry had seen Henrik bounding over a curb and screeching into a parking place, laughing all the way at the shrieks of some girls who were sure he was going to fall. And there was Jorge Perez and Woody Clark and—and who?

"Who is"—Terry paused over the name—"Krystian"— he spoke slowly as he read off the syllables—"Wisniewski?"

Schmidt smiled. "It is pronounced Wiz-nef'-ski. It is a Polish name. His father is with the Polish consulate."

"Polish," Terry said. "You mean, from Poland?"

Schmidt smiled again. "Well, yes, originally. But they have lived all over the world—England for several years before they came to this country."

"Oh," Terry said.

Terry signed his name to the list. As he laid down the pencil, he had a funny feeling in the pit of his stomach. He was leaving the football world he knew and excelled in. He was leaving old friends for new teammates. He was leaving the game he had grown up with for one that he hardly knew existed three years ago. He was leaving certain stardom, stepping out of a spotlight. He was entering the strange new soccer world. Would he find another spotlight?

Then he remembered Hank Dodsworth's familiar line: "It's a beautiful game." Terry agreed. It *was* a beautiful game. He recalled the thrill of the long play for the winning goal in the park-district match and beating Bones Nelson in a one-on-one duel.

Schmidt interrupted Terry's thoughts. "We practice at two o'clock this afternoon, you know," he said.

Terry smiled. "Right," he said. "See you there."

He turned and walked in the direction of Wilson Brundage's office.

Chapter 3

Brundage was alone in his office, seated at his desk and scribbling on a pad of yellow paper, when Terry appeared in the door.

The football coach was a heavyset man, not tall, with the thick neck and brawny forearms of the All-Big-Ten guard he had been at Purdue. Now fifteen years past his last game for Purdue, he still looked fit enough to take the field. His thick, unruly blond hair and face full of freckles gave him an almost gentle countenance, and he looked like everybody's idea of a good guy. The students in his biology classes said that was exactly what he was—a good guy, understanding, friendly, cheerful. Terry never had had a biology course under Brundage, however; he had seen only the fierce competitor of the football field. Apparently Wilson Brundage reserved all his good humor for the classroom and all his wild outbursts of temper for the football field. Having seen the temper in action, Terry was thinking of it when he stepped into the coach's office.

"All ready for the new season, Masters?" Brundage was smiling up at Terry.

Terry shifted his weight from one foot to the other in the doorway.

"You're frowning, Masters. What's wrong?"

Terry wished that Brundage would call him Terry instead of Masters. But Brundage addressed all of his players by their last name. Terry's father had explained that the coach was demonstrating that he considered his players to be young men—men, not boys.

"It's the new season that I want to talk to you about," Terry said.

Brundage still smiled. "C'mon in. Have a seat."

Terry stepped through the door and seated himself on the straight wooden chair alongside the coach's desk. "Coach, I. . . ."

"What's the problem?"

Terry swallowed hard. "I've decided not to play football this year, and I thought that I should be the first to tell you, myself." Terry spoke rapidly. With an effort, he managed to look Brundage in the eye as he did so. "It's not—"

"It's not what?" Brundage was no longer smiling.

"I've decided that I would rather play soccer, and I've signed up for the soccer team."

Brundage leaned back in his chair. He tossed down the pencil on the yellow pad and frowned but said nothing for a moment. Then he got up abruptly, closed his office door, and returned to his chair behind the desk.

Terry stared straight ahead. He braced himself for the explosion that undoubtedly was coming. But it never came.

"I see," Brundage said finally. He spoke softly and slowly, shifting himself in his chair. "Are you sure that this is what you want to do?"

"Yes. I've thought about it a lot."

"You have a brilliant season—a brilliant future—ahead of you in football."

Terry said nothing. Then he murmured, "I've made up my mind."

"Soccer," Brundage said, more to himself than to Terry. He was staring away from Terry, absently rubbing his lower lip with a forefinger.

Terry clenched his teeth. He was sure of what Brundage was going to say next. He would use the old challenge of the football coach to the player who is quitting: "Can't take the hitting, eh? Afraid of a little pain, huh? Decided to give up the contact and go out for a girls' sport, eh?" Terry had heard variations of the line from Brundage often enough on the practice field. What could Terry tell him? He could say no, he was not afraid of the physical pounding of football, which was the truth. But the questions themselves carried a charge hardly refutable by a simple denial. The only real denial was in the action—stick to it, take the punishment. That was the proof you were not afraid. Or Terry could answer the charge with another truth: He was going to enjoy a sport that relied more on skill and less on brute force, a sport with fewer bruises, scrapes, and broken bones. No, he wasn't afraid of being pounded, but he never had enjoyed it. He wouldn't miss the slamming hits and jarring collisions. He might tell Brundage so.

But Brundage did not ask the questions Terry was expecting. Instead, he said, "Is this because you didn't win the Most Valuable Player trophy last season?"

The question caught Terry by surprise. "No," he said softly. Then his frown deepened. He pushed his hair back off his forehead. The question bothered him. Was this what the coach thought? Was this what the football team—and maybe the soccer team, too—were going to think? Sure, he'd been disappointed at the time that he didn't win the trophy, bitterly disappointed. Now, staring into Wilson Brundage's eyes, he told himself quickly that the disappointment had faded into nothing. Then he recalled that only this morning he had been thinking about it. But the loss of the varsity trophy had never entered his mind when he made his decision to leave football for soccer. At least, he didn't think so. "No," he repeated. "Not at all."

Brundage seemed to accept the answer. He watched Terry a moment. Then he asked, "Does your father know of this decision?"

Terry was sure that Brundage already knew the answer. The coach and his father were good friends. His father frequently attended the football practices. The coach even listened to his father's advice about the team on occasion. If Alvin Masters had already known of his son's decision, he would have called Brundage, and Brundage knew it. The two of them would have gone to work immediately to reverse the decision.

"Not yet," Terry said.

"He will be very disappointed, you know."

"Yes, I know," Terry said. "But I'm the one doing the playing, and it was a decision that I had to make for myself, and I've decided that I would rather play soccer than football."

Brundage, frowning slightly, waited without speaking. He seemed to feel he had hit a nerve. He was waiting for the full impact to sink in.

Finally Terry broke the silence. "I thought that I should be the one to tell you of my decision," he said. He hoped that by repeating this statement he was bringing the interview to an end. "I thought that you should hear it first from me."

"Yes, of course," Brundage said. He paused and, again, stared away from Terry. Then, speaking more to himself than to Terry, he said, "I wondered when it would happen, and who it would be."

"What?"

"Nothing," Brundage said. "Nothing at all." He leaned forward in the chair, and Terry got to his feet. Brundage stood up. "Good luck, Terry. If you change your mind, let me know." He extended his hand, and Terry shook it.

Terry left, surprised by Brundage's subdued reaction and puzzled by the mumbled aside: "I wondered when it would happen, and who it would be."

Walking home, Terry was deep in his own thoughts. The burden had been lifted. He had done it. He had signed up for soccer and faced up to Wilson Brundage. He felt a great sense of relief. The hardest part was over, although there were some tough moments still to go. There was his father. There were the football players. But he had made the big step and committed himself.

Terry hardly heard the whirring motor behind him until Henrik Sterner appeared at his side on the ever-present moped.

"You signed up for soccer," Henrik called out.

Terry turned. "Yeah, I sure did," he said.

Henrik, the stalwart of the Eagles' defense the year before, slowed the moped to a crawl alongside Terry. "That's great. We can use some scoring punch up front."

34

Before Terry could reply, Henrik roared away, bouncing over a curb to cut a corner at the expense of somebody's lawn. Terry smiled at the spectacle and thought to himself, Someday somebody is going to shoot out both your tires for that, Henrik, ol' boy.

At home, Terry's mother greeted him at the front door with a raised eyebrow and a low, soft whistle. "Call your father," she said. "He's called you twice in the last twenty minutes."

Wilson Brundage was not giving up. He was wasting no time. The counterattack was under way.

"Did Dad tell you?"

"Yes."

"Well?"

"It's your decision, Terry," she said. Then she smiled. "But do call your father right now, before he calls back again. I'll have lunch on the table for you when you've finished."

"I'll be lucky if I'm off the phone with Dad in time for dinner."

Terry walked into the den and dropped into the heavy, overstuffed chair next to the telephone table. He stared into space a moment, then picked up the telephone and dialed the number of his father's office.

"What is this that Wilson Brundage is telling me?" his father asked.

"It's true," Terry said.

"Terry, you're making a mistake."

"I don't think so."

"Are you sure that you've thought this thing through?"

"Yes."

"You never discussed it with me."

"I knew what you would say."

Terry waited. So far the conversation had gone exactly as he had expected. He knew that his father would be disbelieving at first, then astounded. And, of course, disappointed. But not angry. Terry had seldom seen his father angry. He knew he would not be angry now.

"But soccer. . . ."

Terry took a deep breath. He hoped his father was not going to say the things he had feared Brundage was going to say—"Afraid of a little hitting, eh?" He finally spoke. "Yes, Dad, soccer. It's a beautiful game, Dad. I like soccer more than football. It's more fun. I'd rather play soccer than football. I can't play both of them at the same time, so I'm going to play soccer."

"You're turning your back on a brilliant future in football."

Terry had known he would say that. Alvin Masters was looking forward to seeing another Masters on the All-American football teams. But Terry did not want to be "another Masters." He wanted to be Terry Masters, not "the son of Alvin Masters." Terry never had raised the subject with his father, but it was always in his mind. And certainly one of the great attractions of soccer over football was the

36

knowledge that he would be Terry Masters, not "the son of Alvin Masters."

"Maybe I will have a brilliant future in soccer," Terry said.

There was silence at the other end of the telephone line. Then Terry's father said, "This is a great disappointment to me, you know."

"Yes, I know. And I'm sorry."

Hanging up, Terry sat for a moment with his hand on the telephone. His father did not understand. How could he? His father never had played soccer. His father had never been "the son of Alvin Masters." His father had a dream, another Masters on the All-American football teams. Terry had a different dream, soccer stardom, not football stardom.

The telephone rang under Terry's hand, startling him. He looked at the instrument. The caller was sure to be one of two people—Hank Dodsworth, elated, or Steve Palmer, angry and disappointed. While Terry waited, the telephone rang a second time.

"Are you answering?" Terry's mother called out from the dining room.

"Yes," Terry said. He picked up the receiver. He wondered—Hank or Steve? "Hello," he said.

"Great! Great! Great!" Hank's voice was a gleeful shout coming over the telephone line.

Terry grinned into the telephone. "I was just going to call you," he said.

"Why didn't you tell me before?"

"I really wasn't sure. No, I was sure. But I really couldn't believe it myself. Not until I actually had signed the list."

"Well, you've done it. I knew you would."

"Where did you hear about it?"

"Bones Nelson. I don't know where he heard. He said the word is all over the school. You're the big news story at Windsor High today."

"Bones. . . ." Terry could imagine Bones's reaction to the news. Bones Nelson's days as the star of the Windsor High soccer team were at an end. "What did Bones say?" Terry asked.

"Mostly he just prattled about a Polish guy, Krystian what's-his-name. Do you know him?"

"I saw his name on the list."

"Bones says that he's great, really great."

"Oh? How's he know?"

"Schmidt, I guess. I don't know." Hank paused. "Say, have you got a problem with Bones?"

"Problem? With Bones? I hardly know him. He's a year ahead of us. He never played football or basketball or baseball. He—" Terry stopped. "What do you mean, a problem?"

"After all the talk about Krystian what's-his-name, he said a funny thing."

"What?"

"He said he wondered how you were going to like not being the star for a change."

"He did?"

"You know—football, baseball, basketball."

"Uh-huh."

"I just thought it was a funny remark to make," Hank said. "You know, especially with you and me being good friends."

"Yeah, funny."

"Well, see you at practice."

"Sure."

"Sounds like we're loaded, with you and Krystian what's-his-name added to the team."

"Yeah."

After hanging up, Terry shrugged. He had not told Hank, but he could see the game Bones was playing. If Terry Masters was going to knock Bones Nelson out of the spotlight, Bones would enjoy watching the Polish boy knock Terry out of the spotlight. It would take the superstar down a notch or two. Terry had seen it before. He knew the signs of jealousy. Even among his own teammates, he had observed small glints of satisfaction on occasion when he faltered. Teamwork was important, and the Eagles usually had it in every sport, but Terry sometimes saw signs of envy among those around him. That was part of the price of being the star. Terry always had understood and accepted the price.

"Are you coming to lunch?" his mother called out. "Are you off the telephone?"

"Coming."

Terry's second telephone call followed not long after. He left his lunch half finished to take it.

"I just heard," Steve Palmer said. The quarterback's voice was a mixture of flat disappointment and anger barely controlled. "I couldn't believe it. Do you know what you're doing?"

"Yes."

"I mean, do you know what you're doing to us?"

Terry recalled the summertime talk from Steve and all the others. The Windsor Eagles football team was headed for a sensational season. Everybody was looking toward a championship, perhaps an undefeated season. The running of Terry Masters was an important part of the scenario. Terry knew it. The fact had weighed heavily on him in these last few days when he knew that his decision had been made.

"Steve, this was not an easy decision for me." Terry spoke slowly and distinctly. He had carefully rehearsed the words in his own mind. "It was a decision I could not escape. The reasons all boil down to one thing: I want to play soccer instead of football. I like soccer more than I like football. That's all there is to it."

The telephone line was silent for a moment. "We were counting on you."

"I know."

Then, finally, his lunch finished, it was time to return to school for the first practice with the soccer team.

Chapter 4

Terry bounded down the stairs toward the dressing room in the basement of Windsor High. He carried his soccer shoes in his right hand. At the bottom of the flight of stairs, he stopped for a moment. Down the hall to his right, in the other dressing room, he could hear the chatter and shouts of the football players. They were checking out their equipment and pulling on their practice uniforms for the first drill of the season.

For an instant, Terry felt again the twinge of uncertainty. It was the same feeling he had experienced when he signed the soccer clipboard just a few hours before. He was leaving a world that he knew. The rapid sequence of the day's events tumbled through his mind briefly—the strange reaction of Wilson Brundage, the disappointment of his father, the bitterness of Steve Palmer, even Hank's question about a problem with Bones Nelson. Terry frowned at the recollection.

Then he slapped his thigh with the soccer shoes in his right hand, shoved open the door to the dressing room with his left hand, and stepped inside.

"Hey! There he is!" Hank Dodsworth called out from a spot at a locker where he was hanging up his shirt.

Terry smiled and waved at Hank.

Bones Nelson, already in his practice uniform, looked up from tying a shoe. For a moment, Terry thought Bones wasn't going to speak. Bones seemed to be measuring Terry. Then he smiled and said, "Welcome aboard. Glad to have you."

"Thanks." Terry managed a smile in return.

Horst Schmidt walked by. "Over here, Terry, for your uniform and locker assignment," he said. Schmidt was not the smiling, chatty person he had been at the sign-up table this morning. The change neither surprised nor puzzled Terry. He had seen the two faces of other coaches. Off the field, away from the game, they were friendly and affable, even fun. But at work, on the field or in the dressing room, they were straight-faced, serious, almost grim. Horst

Schmidt was the same as the others. To coaches, coaching was serious business.

"Sure," Terry said, turning to follow Schmidt.

Heading for the equipment table, Schmidt glanced back at the shoes in Terry's hand. "You've got shoes," he said. "Good."

Terry knew that the soccer players were required to furnish their own playing shoes.

Schmidt walked around the table and shoved across a wire basket containing a practice uniform and a game uniform. A locker key, with identifying number, dangled from the top rim of the basket.

"You told Brundage this morning," Schmidt said suddenly.

The remark—a statement of fact, not a question—caught Terry by surprise. "Yes," he said finally. He wondered how Schmidt knew. Had Brundage told him? Then he wondered why Schmidt bothered to mention it at all. Did he want to know Brundage's reaction? "Yes, I did. I told him."

"I saw you walking toward his office and assumed you felt you should tell him of your decision yourself," Schmidt said. "That was the correct thing to do."

Terry paused. Then he said, "Coach Brundage made a funny remark when I told him."

"Funny? How is that?"

"He said he had wondered when it would happen, and who it would be. He didn't explain what he meant."

Schmidt smiled slightly. "I know what he meant," he said. "I know exactly what he meant."

"Yes?"

The arrival of Jorge Perez interrupted them. Jorge, an exchange student from Guatemala, played halfback. His expert passing and surefooted dribbling were valuable at midfield. Terry had heard Hank alternately rave and moan about Jorge. Skilled as only a lifelong soccer player can be, Jorge frequently was the best all-around player on the field when the Eagles played a match. But his weight kept him from reaching his full potential as a soccer player. His abilities, great as they were, foundered under the excess fat he carried from his puffy cheeks to his ankles. On the field, he was slow—too slow—and he tired quickly. More than once, when his skills were needed in the closing minutes of a tight match, Jorge was to be found panting on the sideline while a substitute played in his place. By Hank's estimate, two matches the Eagles lost the previous season might have been won if Jorge had not run out of steam in the final period.

"Jorge, did you spend the summer running up those mountains in Guatemala as I told you to do?"

Jorge grinned sheepishly. "A little," he said.

Schmidt did not smile. Jorge's appearance told the tale. Jorge had run up the mountains very little. Schmidt said, "Well, we'll see, won't we?"

"Yes, sir." Jorge took his basket and moved along the row of lockers, looking at the numbers.

44

Terry waited.

Schmidt watched Jorge a moment and then turned back to Terry.

"Terry, though soccer is a relatively minor sport at Windsor High, it is the major one around the world. In this country, in the ethnic neighborhoods of the big cities, soccer is also the major sport. Henrik, you know, grew up playing soccer in his German neighborhood in the city, and Hank played soccer in St. Louis. But in most American high schools the outstanding athletes have always chosen football." Schmidt paused. "Until now, that's certainly been true at Windsor High," he said. "Terry, you are the first outstanding athlete here to choose soccer over football. Coach Brundage knew that the day was coming, but he did not know when or who the first one would be. Now he knows, and that is what he meant."

Terry nodded. It made sense. Terry never had considered himself anything but an outstanding athlete in any of the sports he played. He shoved his hair back off his forehead and grinned at Schmidt. "So we're making history, huh?" he said.

Schmidt gave Terry a tight little smile. "You'd better get dressed for practice," he said.

Terry found his locker next to Chuck Horton, a senior who played fullback, and began peeling off his clothes to change into his practice uniform.

"I heard you were coming out for soccer," Chuck said.

"That's great." Chuck, like Bones Nelson and Henrik Sterner, played no other sport and managed to play soccer in one form or another—school varsity or park district—almost year-round. "We can use you," Chuck said.

Terry grinned at Chuck. "I can hardly wait to get going," he said.

Behind him, Terry heard the door open and close. Somebody else had arrived.

Chuck, dressed and seated on the bench, leaning back against the locker, said, "That must be the new Polish guy."

Terry turned and looked at Krystian what's-his-name. He was smaller than Terry, probably about five feet nine inches tall, weighing maybe a hundred and fifty pounds. He had the same sort of packed in, taut physique as Horst Schmidt, and Terry figured he was probably heavier and stronger than he looked.

"Come in, Krystian," Schmidt said from the table where he was issuing uniforms and locker keys. Then, to the room as a whole, he said, "All of you know each other except for this one newcomer. This is Krystian Wisniewski. He's new to Windsor and new to the United States, but he's an experienced soccer player. He played in his native Poland and in England, where his family lived for several years."

Krystian smiled easily and gave a little nod.

"Bones, you met Krystian at the sign-up table this morning," Schmidt said. "Why don't you introduce him around?"

Schmidt turned back to Krystian. "This basket contains your practice uniform and your game uniform, and this is your locker key."

"I must apologize for being late," Krystian said. His English was thickly accented, but he did not stumble over the words. Obviously, he knew the language. The Polish accent was natural enough, but Terry was surprised by the traces of an English accent. Then Terry remembered that Krystian had lived in England before coming to the United States. "I went to the wrong dressing room and got mixed up," Krystian said.

Bones, standing next to him, grinned and said, "I'll bet I know what happened."

"I asked this boy in the passageway above where the football dressing room was located, and he said, 'Follow me, that's where I'm headed,' and I followed him, and—"

The laughter from all around the dressing room stopped Krystian in midsentence. All of the players knew that in every other part of the world soccer was called football.

Krystian shrugged and grinned.

"He almost wound up with the head knockers," Bones howled.

Everybody laughed again.

Bones began making the rounds of the dressing room, quickly introducing Krystian to each of the players. "You won't remember all the names right away," he said.

When they reached Terry, Bones said, "Masters used to

be a big star with the head knockers, but he's decided to play soccer this year."

The words "a big star," and the way the words were spoken, caused Terry to turn to Bones. He eyed Bones for a moment. Hank had asked if Terry had a problem with Bones. Terry had asked himself the same question when he and Bones had stared at each other, unspeaking, just a few minutes ago. And now the question popped up again. Terry wanted to ask Bones, "What's with you?" But instead he turned back to Krystian. "Welcome to Windsor," he said. Krystian smiled. "Thank you," he said, moving on behind Bones. Terry finished dressing.

Suddenly the door flew open, and Henrik Sterner stood there, red-faced, huffing and panting. Everyone turned and stared. "Am I late?" Henrik blurted.

"You are late," Schmidt said.

"My moped blew a tire."

The sight of Henrik, wide-eyed and breathing heavily, and the vision of his moped blowing a tire sent the room into gales of laughter again.

"That's good," Chuck Horton called out from his spot on the bench next to Terry. "Maybe the women and children will be safer on the streets with you off the thing, and maybe you won't break a leg before the season even gets started."

Henrik looked hurt.

"Get dressed, Henrik," Schmidt said, shoving a basket across the table. "We're ready to go to the field."

48

Chapter 5

"If you work hard, we have good reason to hope for an outstanding season," Horst Schmidt was saying.

The players were sprawled out on the ground in a semi-circle around the coach. Schmidt, wearing khaki trousers, a gray sweatshirt, and a blue baseball cap, was down on one knee, his elbow resting on the other knee. He was talking to the players—eighteen of them—before they moved onto the field to begin their first practice session.

The soccer team's practice field was a large expanse of lawn alongside the Episcopal Church, two blocks from the school, with portable goals set up at the north and south ends. It was unhandy to the dressing room, but it was the best arrangement the school could make when soccer had been decreed to be a varsity sport. The soccer team played its matches on the varsity football field, but they could not practice there. Not even the football team practiced on the manicured turf where the games were played but used a field on the school grounds behind the west bleachers.

"We have lost little—very little—from last year's team," Schmidt said. "Those of you who are returning are a year older. You are a little quicker, a little stronger than last year. You are more experienced than last year. You have sharpened your skills. You will be better soccer players this year than last year."

Schmidt glanced at the players in the semicircle around him, as if he were counting in his mind the starters returning from last year's team. Three were seniors—Henrik Sterner, Chuck Horton, and Bones Nelson—heading into their final season at Windsor High. Three were juniors who had made the starting lineup as sophomores last year— Hank Dodsworth, Jorge Perez, and Woody Clark.

Others, while not starters last season, had seen a lot of playing action—Bob Traynor, Paul Chandler, Archie McAlister, Butch Sterling.

Terry lay back on the grass, braced on his elbows, his legs straight out and spread apart, watching the coach. Next to Terry, Hank was sitting cross-legged.

50

"We are fortunate, too," Schmidt said, "in having added soccer strength joining the team this year."

Schmidt's statement took Terry's mind back a half hour to the conversation with the coach in the dressing room. "You are the first outstanding athlete here to choose soccer over football," Schmidt had said. Unconsciously, Terry was awaiting a meaningful glance from the coach.

Terry was used to being singled out. He had starred in football, first on the freshman team and then on the varsity. He had been a leading scorer on the basketball team last season. He had batted clean-up on the baseball team. Now he was going to be a star on the soccer team. Coaches always had acknowledged Terry Masters's presence and his importance to the team. Terry was used to the spotlight. And he knew how to handle himself in its bright glare.

But Horst Schmidt was looking at Krystian Wisniewski when he spoke. "We have Krystian joining the team," Schmidt said, "and he brings to us a lot of soccer experience."

Terry flushed as a wave of embarrassment swept over him. He had been ready to acknowledge with a small smile, a slight nod, the coach's recognition of his importance to the team. Instead, Terry kept his eyes on the coach, hoping Schmidt would not look at him. He did not want to meet Horst Schmidt's gaze at this moment. He hoped that Hank, seated next to him, was not looking at him. He hoped that none of the others—Bones Nelson, Henrik Sterner, Chuck Horton, none of them—were looking at him at this moment.

Terry glanced quickly at Krystian. Krystian was nodding slightly in acknowledgment. Terry knew the gesture. He had used it often enough himself.

"And Terry Masters is new to the team, coming over from the football team," Schmidt said.

Terry looked back at the coach.

"We all know of Terry's abilities from the park-district soccer play during the summer," Schmidt finished.

Schmidt glanced at Terry, and Terry nodded slightly.

Schmidt was saying something else now. But Terry did not hear the words. They came through to him as a murmur, undiscernable. He hardly saw the coach kneeling there at the opening in the semicircle of players. The shade cast over the players by the giant old elm tree at the edge of the playing field seemed suddenly to darken. For the first time in his life, Terry Masters was sharing the spotlight with another player. Worse yet, Terry did not even rate the top billing.

Schmidt was getting to his feet now. The players were getting up too. Terry rolled over onto his stomach and sprang to his feet.

"The Polish guy must really be something," Hank said softly, almost in a whisper.

Terry glared at Hank. "I don't know," he said. "Who's seen him play?"

Hank glanced at Terry. "Well, he's European, and you know. . . ."

Terry knew. Jorge Perez, coming from another part of the world where soccer was the major sport, was a good example of the skills that come with a lifetime of playing the game.

Schmidt emptied the huge bag of soccer balls he had brought to the field in the trunk of his car. Players moved in, picked off the balls with their feet, and dribbled onto the field.

Immediately any mystery about Krystian Wisniewski vanished. The first instant he took control of a ball the story was clear. The next few minutes only served as confirmation. Terry and the others found themselves gawking in fascination.

Dribbling, Krystian seemed to make the ball an extension of his feet. He seemed able to *will* the movements of the ball. The ball was a *part* of Krystian Wisniewski, and it did his bidding. Left foot or right made no difference to Krystian.

He was not an exceptionally fast player. But he had a quickness about him that Terry had never seen in the soccer players around Windsor. He had, too, a knack of changing pace intuitively, leaving baffled defenders behind, alone, confused, and chagrined. His passes hit the mark every time. His headers were as accurate as his passes.

As a defender, Krystian showed that he had more speed with his feet than one might have guessed. He tackled neatly, cleanly, confidently—and effectively. He was also aggressive, knifing in and deftly taking the ball away from

53

a hapless opponent. Clearly, for any of the Eagles, a duel with Krystian Wisniewski was a lost cause.

Just as important as his skills was the fact that Krystian never stopped working. He was constantly on the move, either pursuing an opponent with the ball or weaving into the open space to take a pass from a teammate. Terry had heard his coach in the park district league say a thousand times: "Go for the open space, go where the open space is going to be." Krystian did. He seemed to anticipate the open spots on the field. What had been a crowd suddenly dissolved into nothing but Krystian, open again for a pass. He knew what to look for on the field, and he sped to the spot.

"I think he's played this game before," puffed Woody Clark, the junior fullback. Woody was recovering from a frantic—and futile—effort to stop Krystian from dribbling around him.

Among the Eagles, only two—Henrik Sterner and Jorge Perez—came even close to being Krystian's match. Henrik, the senior sweeper, having grown up in a German neighborhood in Chicago, had played soccer all his life. He was a tough defender, and it took a tough one to compete with Krystian. Jorge was another lifelong soccer player, able and skilled, but too heavy and slow to keep up with Krystian.

Terry tangled with the dribbling Krystian once. Quick and strong, Terry stayed with him long enough to say he had bothered him, then lost him. Another time, when Terry had the ball, he barely got off a pass before Krystian had blocked it.

Horst Schmidt, standing at the touchline, smiled at the Polish boy's dazzling demonstration. He seemed to be seeing something off in the future that pleased him. Or maybe he was thinking back to other, better days of his own on the playing fields of the world. Horst Schmidt was a fierce competitor. He had worked his way out of a small town in Germany to the pinnacle of world-class soccer and then seen it all come crashing down in a single tragic moment of collision on the playing field. He was through, his own playing days ended. But now Horst Schmidt looked as if he were sniffing the lovely aroma of victory again. Horst Schmidt was going to be a winner once more.

For Terry Masters, there were other thoughts. He could see that his days of being the brightest star on the field were at an end.

Chapter 6

The ten days of practice leading up to the opening match flew by for Terry.

The drills twice a day, in the morning and again in the afternoon, kept him busy. He was too busy for anything other than the demands of soccer. He had not seen Wilson Brundage or any of his former football teammates since sign-up day. The football players were busy with their own twice-a-day drills at their field two blocks away from the soccer practice field. And the evenings, when Terry might have encountered Steve Palmer or any of the others at

Herbie's Place or some such popular spot around town, Terry spent at home, going to bed early. In all likelihood, the football players were doing the same. Terry knew from experience that their weariness was as great as his.

On the practice field, Terry was too busy with the tasks at hand to worry about Krystian Wisniewski moving into the spotlight with him. Terry had plenty to learn and precious little time to do so. Under the watchful eye of Horst Schmidt, he discovered new aspects of the game every day. Schmidt had lessons to teach that the volunteer coach in the park-district league either never knew or did not bother to mention. In addition, Terry had to absorb the tactics, the strategy, the philosophy of Horst Schmidt's style of soccer. The combination was a full-time assignment.

But he could not help feeling a sense of relief when it became clear that Krystian was destined to play halfback, while Terry was certain to play forward. There was no announcement. From the start, Schmidt said little about who was going to play where and even less about who would win the starting positions. All the players got a taste of all the positions in the early days of the drills. Schmidt was shaking down the squad, testing various combinations. But by the fifth day of practice, Krystian was spending most of his time at halfback, and Terry was playing almost exclusively at forward. The thought flitted unbidden through Terry's mind one day: Krystian at halfback, Terry at forward. They were not competing for the same position in the lineup.

They were not competing for playing time in the matches. Krystian was not a factor at all in Terry's drive to win a starting position. If there was to be any competition between them on the field, it would be for the role of star, which Terry was used to having for himself.

Terry was surprised when, on that very same day, Krystian jogged up alongside him on the two-block walk to the dressing room after the long afternoon's practice. The late-summer sun was low in the sky, touching the top of the trees lining Waddington Road across from the practice field, and Terry was ready for an end to the afternoon's work and for his second shower of the day.

"I can't believe that you have never played soccer before," Krystian said.

Terry, wiping the perspiration from his face with a towel, turned with a start. Krystian's thick Polish accent, with the odd overlay of British English, had surprised him.

"Huh?" Terry said.

"You play very well," Krystian said, falling into step with Terry. He was smiling at him. "It is difficult to believe that you never played the game before."

"I played a couple of summers in the park-district league."

"The park-district league? What is that?"

Terry smiled slightly. For a moment, he found it difficult to describe the park district to a foreigner. "The park district—the public parks—they have a lot of activities for the kids in the summer, and one of them is soccer."

"Ah, I see."

Terry looked at Krystian. It was impossible not to like him. On that first day of practice—at the moment of his embarrassment—Terry was sure that he was not going to like the newcomer. But he had to respect Krystian's playing ability. That much was certain in the first minute on the practice field. And, as the twice-a-day drills rolled by, Terry found himself responding to Krystian's quick smile, his readiness to applaud a good play, his unselfishness in backing up teammates and passing off to them. Krystian seemed aloof, to be sure. But Terry was beginning to think that Krystian's apparent aloofness was, in fact, just the shyness of a newcomer. And now he was going out of his way to compliment Terry's abilities on the soccer field.

"And you," Terry said, "I guess that you've played soccer all your life."

Krystian smiled and nodded. "I cannot remember not playing soccer," he said.

"It shows," Terry said, a little surprised at himself. He was more accustomed to being admired than admiring.

"We're going to have a good team," Krystian said.

They reached the school building and walked through the basement door. The coolness in the basement corridor felt good to Terry. He wondered, as they walked toward the dressing room, if Krystian felt relief that one of them was a halfback and the other a forward. But he already knew the answer: No. Krystian Wisniewski seemed to feel no rivalry at all with his teammates. The thought made Terry frown.

59

They pushed their way through the doors into the dressing room and parted, each heading for his own locker.

"See you later."

"Yeah."

Bones Nelson, though, remained cool—at times almost hostile—toward Terry as the players ground their way through the preseason drills. Terry had little time in the heat of the twice-a-day sessions to worry about him, however, until the end of the eighth day of practice. He and Hank Dodsworth were walking home together.

"Does it bother you, Krystian being such a good player?" Hank asked.

The question, coming out of the blue, startled Terry. "Wha-a-a-t? What do you mean?"

"Bones says it does."

"Bones. . . ."

"Says he knew it from the start."

"What in the world are you talking about?"

"Look, I'm not trying to make trouble. But—"

"But what?" Terry glared at Hank. Terry and Hank had been close friends for two years, since they first met as members of the freshman baseball team. The two of them, both superior athletes, had become fast friends almost immediately. At one time, Terry had tried to talk Hank into coming out for football. With his agility and reach, Hank was a natural pass receiver. In the end, however, Hank was the one who had lured Terry over to another sport. "But what?" Terry repeated.

"Well, you couldn't have helped noticing how Bones has been acting toward you. You know, sort of cool, and all that."

"Bones doesn't like the idea of not being the only forward who can score. He's afraid that I'll knock some of the shine off him. He's jealous, that's all." They walked in silence for a moment. Then Terry said, "And I will knock the shine off him."

Hank said nothing. He seemed sorry he had brought up the subject.

"But you started to say something," Terry said. "Something about what Bones was saying."

"I think you ought to know."

"Ought to know what?"

"Bones says that you've always been the big star of the team in every sport you've played—and I guess that's true, isn't it?—and that you won't be able to stand not being the star of the soccer team."

"Because of Bones?"

"No, because of Krystian."

"That's what Bones meant on sign-up day, isn't it?"

"Yes, I guess he already knew about Krystian, and he thought—"

"I *like* Krystian."

"Everybody does, but—"

"Besides, Krystian is a halfback. I'm a forward. Krystian is supposed to control the center of the field. I'm supposed to score. So what's the problem?"

Hank's quick glance sent Terry's mind back to his moment of relief when he realized that he and Krystian would not be playing the same position, that they were competing only for the starring role.

"You and I don't interfere with each other," Terry continued. "We play different positions. Krystian and I won't interfere with each other. We play different positions. Bones is just jealous."

"Yeah," Hank said finally. "Maybe you're right." But he didn't sound sure of it.

"He's just jealous," Terry repeated.

The night of the Eagles' first match of the season, the Thursday before the Labor Day weekend, was clear and warm. The Eagles were playing on their home field, taking on the Henderson Park Panthers.

Stepping onto the field for the loosening-up drills, Terry looked at the familiar scene of the Windsor High football field.

Familiar? No, not really. The bleachers were strangely empty. For a football game, the crowd was sure to be overflowing, noisy with enthusiasm. But for this soccer match the crowd consisted of small groups of people scattered through the bleacher seats on one side of the field. They were the parents and friends of the players, with a few curious students and townspeople mixed in for a look at the strange sport. Soccer at Windsor High was still too new to have gained widespread following among the fans, and the Eagles' lackluster record of last year had done little to spark excitement.

Even the way the players entered the arena was unfamiliar to Terry. For a football team, the entry was high drama, the captain leading the charging throng, all armored for the battle, through a corridor of shouting cheerleaders, bringing the people in the bleachers to their feet with a roar. But the soccer players, once dressed in their game uniforms, ambled casually out onto the field, chatting among themselves, hardly noticed by the fans dotting the one side of the bleachers opened to the public.

Halfway up the field toward the bench, Terry and the others slowed their pace and watched the Henderson Park Panthers, already on the field, racing through their warm-up drills.

Terry eyed the opposing players carefully. He was looking for a talent to match Krystian, or Bones—or himself. "They don't look like much," he said.

Bones turned. "That's what we thought last year when we met them in the opener," he said.

Hank, beside Terry, let out a long, exaggerated moan. "Don't mention it," he said. "It was my first match as a starter, and they beat us 4–2. My first start as goalie, and I gave up four goals. Please don't mention it."

"That's right, you did," Henrik Sterner piped up with a devilish leer on his face. "I had forgotten."

Krystian kept his eyes on the Henderson Park players at the other end of the field, hardly paying attention to the banter among his teammates. As he watched, a confident expression appeared on his face: the look of a superior player sizing up an opponent and finding nothing to worry about.

No, Terry thought, the Eagles have nothing to worry about tonight. The message was clearly written on Krystian Wisniewski's face.

Past the players and beyond the nets of the soccer goal, Terry saw the football goalposts standing in place. For a moment he felt a wave of nostalgia for the game he had left behind.

Horst Schmidt, waiting for the players at the bench, seemed to read Terry's mind. "Terry," he called out.

Terry turned toward the coach.

Schmidt booted a ball toward Terry. Terry stepped forward and stopped the pass with his left foot. Then he dribbled toward the center of the field. The other players picked off balls and moved out in a weaving crowd to begin the warm-up drills.

Through the carefully structured routine of the warm-up drills—dribbling, dueling, shooting—Terry caught the Henderson Park coach watching him. Terry Masters was a new element on the Windsor team. He was added firepower, a known quantity from his park-district play. Terry booted a line-drive shot into Hank's hands at the goal and turned to jog back to his place in line. The Henderson Park coach was looking at someone else now—the slender lad with black hair, a stranger who wore number 15, Krystian Wisniewski.

Down the sideline, Horst Schmidt stood with arms folded, staring at his team from under the bill of the baseball cap. He glared at each player taking his turn at shooting on goal, saying nothing, showing nothing.

The referee blew his whistle. The Eagles from their end of the field and the Panthers from their end converged on their benches. The match was about to begin.

Schmidt was holding a piece of paper in his hand, the starting lineup, to be read off and then delivered to the officials.

Terry's heart skipped a beat. Neither he nor any of the other players knew the names written on that piece of paper. Never once during the ten days of preseason practice had Horst Schmidt even hinted who might—and who might not—be on the starting lineup for the first match of the season. Terry figured some of the players to be cinches. Hank would get the nod at goalie. Bones Nelson and Henrik Sterner and Chuck Horton were returning as starters from last year's team. Nobody was going to knock them off the lineup. Krystian Wisniewski, with the quick feet, the sure passes, was certain to be a starter.

But Terry Masters?

Horst Schmidt had told Terry on sign-up day, "We will

be glad to have you on the team. The Eagles can use your abilities." But that was a far distance from the promise of a place on the starting lineup.

Terry knew that he could outplay them all, Bones Nelson, Archie McAlister, Butch Sterling, at the forward position. He had proved it in the preseason practice.

But Terry knew, too, that coaches sometimes played games with the starting lineup. Bones was a certainty for one of the forward slots, no question. He was the leading scorer of the team last year. That left either Archie or Butch to sit on the bench if Terry got the nod. Both had been on the squad last year. Terry had not. What if Horst Schmidt awarded the starting position to the veterans of last year's team, feeling he owed them a shot at nailing down the position?

The thought sent a chill through Terry. He could imagine the remarks of the football players, if any of them were up there in the bleachers: "Did you hear that? Masters didn't make the starting lineup." He could imagine the thoughts of his father, watching his son step back and take a seat on the bench at the start of the match.

"All right," Schmidt said. "Here is the way we start."

Schmidt began reading. "Dodsworth at goalie . . . Sterner at sweeper. . . ." The coach was beginning at the back line. "Clark at right fullback . . . Horton at center fullback . . . Traynor at left fullback. . . ."

The referee moved around the outside of the circle of

players, checking their cleats. He would allow no signs of wear on the hard rubber cleats, for then dangerous spikes of metal might become exposed. The procedure was standard in the final moments before a match. As the referee made his way around the circle, players unconsciously lifted one foot, then the other, for inspection.

Schmidt was still reading. "Chandler at right halfback . . . Wisniewski at center halfback . . . Perez at left halfback. . . ."

Terry clenched and unclenched his fists.

"McAlister at right forward . . . Nelson at center forward . . . Masters at left forward."

Terry sighed.

He saw Butch Sterling, downcast, turn back toward the bench to take a seat. Terry turned and ran onto the playing field to take up his position for the start of the match.

Five rows up on the seats directly behind the players' benches, Terry spotted his father, sitting forward, an elbow on his knee and his chin resting on the heel of his hand, staring at the playing field.

Chapter 7

Jorge Perez put the ball into play at the center spot, sending a short pass back to Krystian. The match was on.

Krystian took in the pass with his right foot. Behind Krystian, the fullbacks—Chuck in the center, Woody and Bob at the sides—were up close, the first line of defense in case of a steal or a pass interception at midfield. Farther back, Henrik watched from his sweeper position, ready to support the fullbacks and challenge any opponent breaking through with the ball. He was the last ditch of the defense in front of Hank in the goal mouth.

Alongside Krystian at midfield, Jorge at left halfback

and Paul at right halfback moved ahead, adding pressure to the Eagles' first drive toward the Henderson Park goal.

Up front, Terry was smiling as he and Bones and Archie moved slightly to meet the advance of Krystian with the ball.

From Krystian's first expert tap of the ball, then his smooth dribble around a challenging Henderson Park defender, there was an electricity in the air. The tingling awareness of impending success swept over Terry. Victory was in the making. Terry had experienced the feeling on the football field, on the basketball court, on the baseball diamond. Now he felt it on the soccer field, and it was exhilarating.

The faces of the Henderson Park players showed their concern, wariness turning to alarm almost immediately. The newcomer at center halfback for the Windsor Eagles was a formidable force. Something new and dangerous—and unexpected—was in the lineup for the Windsor Eagles. This was not the Windsor High team that Henderson Park had whipped so handily last season.

Furthermore, in front of the stranger, at the left forward position, stood Terry Masters. Terry was more a known quantity than Krystian. From his football days, the Henderson Park players had reason to be aware that Terry was an outstanding athlete. In addition, in two summers of park-district play, Terry had built a reputation in the suburbs as a talented soccer player. He was also a dangerous new weapon in the Windsor High attack.

In that opening moment, the message was clear: No matches had been won. No goals had been scored. But already the Windsor Eagles, only an average team last year, were a power in the Northwest Suburban Conference this year. Windsor's newfound power was there, obvious and unmistakable, in the opening seconds of the match.

"We're the Windsor Eagles," Terry said to himself, as he had murmured dozens of times before on the football field, the basketball court, the baseball diamond.

From his right, Terry heard Bones unconsciously saying, "Let's go."

Krystian, moving easily, eluded a tackler and sent a short pass skittering over to Paul at right halfback. Paul stopped the ball with his right foot and looked around. He was getting his bearings. But the delay came close to being fatal. A Henderson Park tackler came charging in on Paul. Paul turned, dribbled a couple of yards, almost lost control of the ball, and finally got off a return pass back to Krystian.

Terry and Bones faded back, and Archie moved a couple of steps toward Krystian, positioning themselves for the play that Horst Schmidt had specified for the opening gambit.

Krystian, ten yards from the center circle now and moving to his right, took in the pass from Paul smoothly. He dribbled a few steps back to his left, toward the center of the field, then stopped. He seemed to be looking back to his right, toward Archie. Suddenly he turned and booted a long, low pass to Terry at left forward.

The daring kick caught the Henderson Park defenders out of position and heading the wrong way. A well-coached team, they knew that nobody on a team coached by Horst Schmidt would uncork a long cross-field kick on the first attack of the match. Horst Schmidt and his Windsor Eagles played a conservative game. They were heavily weighted on defense, cautious on offense. They preferred the methodical style of play—short dribbles, short passes, always carefully performed. They played the style of the European teams that Horst Schmidt grew up with. The Windsor Eagles never, never raced wildly up and down the field, kicking for distance and praying for a lucky break. They never opened a match with a gambler's shot—a long cross-field kick.

But there it was—a long line drive cross-field to the left forward.

The Henderson Park defenders, moving toward midfield to meet the threat of Krystian with the ball, slammed on the brakes, screeched to a halt, and turned. Racing back, they took up the defense deep in their own territory.

Terry, alone in the corner, raised his leg and took in Krystian's pass on the inside of his knee. Then he trapped the ball on the ground with his left foot. Bones Nelson dodged around in quick, jerky little motions at the edge of the penalty area, trying to keep himself open.

The Henderson Park goalie, following the flight of the

ball, shifted his position in the goal mouth to face the threat from Terry. Quickly Terry dribbled out from the corner, approaching the edge of the penalty area.

The play called for Terry to make a fast decision. He had three options. If he saw a clear channel past the goalie and into the net, he could shoot for goal. But the anxious goalie was looming large in front of him. If Terry had no room for a shot, he could pass off to Bones. He cast a quick glance at the little center forward. Bones was open, ten yards out from the goal mouth, waving his hands for a pass. Bones looked wide open for a shot, but the Henderson Park defenders were rushing in to cover him, and a fullback was between Bones and the goal, ready to challenge him. Bones was not going to be open for a shot at that spot in another moment or two. Terry's third option was a pass to Krystian, now racing toward the penalty area.

Terry held the ball with his left foot. There was a chance that Bones, asking for the ball, would draw the goalie's attention. The goalie would move away from Terry and turn to Bones, in anticipation of a pass to him. Then Terry would have an open channel to the goal mouth for a shot. But the goalie did not turn. There was a chance that Krystian, charging in, would attract the goalie's attention. The goalie would turn to meet the threat of Krystian. Then Terry would have a clear shot on goal. But the goalie did not turn. He loomed in front of Terry.

Time was running out. The Henderson Park fullbacks were swooping in on Terry. He waited only another fraction of a second. Then his right foot swung through. He caught the ball with his instep and sent a pass rocketing into an open area in front of the advancing Krystian.

Kristian stopped the ball with his left foot, whirled and booted the ball with his right foot into the goal, beyond the frantic lunge of the confused Henderson Park goalie. Terry threw his hands into the air and leaped high with a shout.

The scoreboard blinked: Windsor 1, Visitors 0.

Above the scoreboard, the clock showed the game to be forty-two seconds old. In the bleachers, the small crowd of fans stood and cheered.

Bones grabbed Krystian in a bear hug of congratulations. Paul Chandler and Archie McAlister raced over and clapped him on the back. Terry watched Krystian. He was smiling. He kept shouting to his teammates, *"Tak! Tak!"*—the Polish word for yes, which all of them had heard from him so many times on the practice field. Some of the players were shouting the word back at him in their glee.

Unconsciously Terry glanced at Horst Schmidt at the sideline. Terry was used to the histrionics of Wilson Brundage on the sideline at a game. A touchdown sent the football coach into a spasm of excitement shooting his fists into the air and cheering. Terry himself had been the stimulus for the wild cheering act more than once with a run across the goal for a touchdown.

But Horst Schmidt at the sideline did not cheer the goal. He did not smile or even change expression. Instead, he nodded curtly, as if acknowledging to himself that the play had worked exactly as he had known it would.

The Henderson Park goalie booted the ball, resuming the play, and Terry turned and raced upfield toward the melee.

By half time the Eagles were leading the Panthers by a 5–0 score, and Horst Schmidt already was shuffling substitutes into the game. Butch Sterling replaced Terry. Jorge Perez, winded and perspiring profusely, came off the field for a few minutes of much-needed rest. Krystian stayed in, as did Bones.

Walking off the field toward the dressing room for intermission, Horst Schmidt came alongside Terry. "You frightened me on that opening play," he said.

Terry glanced at the coach. He said nothing.

"You held the ball too long. You almost got caught with it."

Terry stared straight ahead. If the goalie had taken the bait—Bones waiting for a pass, Krystian coming in fast —Terry would have had the goal. He had wanted to score the goal himself. Anyone would. Did Horst Schmidt blame him for wanting to score? "I know," he said finally. Then he added, "But I got the pass away."

74

"Yes," Schmidt said.

In the second half, despite the steady stream of substitutes, the Eagles continued to roll over the Panthers, now sputtering in frustration.

At the forward slots, Terry and Bones, despite their personal feelings, functioned like the two perfect parts of a brilliantly geared machine. Terry's strength and Bones's quickness combined to control the area in front of the Henderson Park goal.

But Krystian was the one, staying in the match almost all the way, who was the key to the Eagles' success. His dominance of the midfield thwarted the Panthers at every turn and set loose the Eagles' drive for goal time and again. As a defender, Krystian seemed to be everywhere, tackling, dueling, challenging at every moment. If the ball was there, Krystian was there. On the attack, Krystian was a stabilizing factor. And, with Bones and Terry flanking him, the Eagles were virtually unstoppable.

In the end, the score was 9–0, the most lopsided soccer match Terry had ever played. Krystian finished with three goals. Bones marked up two goals. Terry got two, one of them on a header off a perfect corner kick by Krystian. Archie McAlister got one on a short shot from the side. Paul Chandler added the final goal on a zany shot out of a tangle of arms and legs at the edge of the penalty area.

Terry's father was waiting for him outside the dressing

room. "I could hear all the shouting in there," he said.

"Yeah," Terry said.

They walked toward the car parked in the lot across the street from the school.

Terry, in the flush of the overwhelming victory, and his part in the victory—the two goals, plus three assists—had joined in the wild shouting in the dressing room.

He had listened to Horst Schmidt when the coach finally waved the cheering players into silence. "You played well, and you won big," he said. Another roaring cheer erupted. Schmidt waved the players into silence again. "But remember," he said, "this was not the best team you will play this season."

Henrik shouted, "Boo! Hiss!" and everyone laughed.

Bones started chanting, "Wiz the Whiz, Wiz the Whiz." The other players picked it up.

Terry glanced at Krystian. He was smiling slightly, with a perplexed expression on his face. "What's a whiz?" he asked.

"You're a whiz," Bones exclaimed.

Terry grinned, but he could not shake off a strange, uneasy feeling. The unpleasant fact was that he, Terry Masters, was outside the spotlight. The glare of stardom was on Krystian Wisniewski. Nobody was cheering Terry Masters, and he could not help noticing. Sure, he had been in other games when a teammate's outstanding play won the loudest cheers. But always before Terry knew that he had had the cheers earlier and would have them again. He was a star. He knew it. Until now.

"Say," Terry's father said, when they were in the car and rolling through the darkened streets of Windsor toward home, "that Polish boy—what's his name?—is one whale of a player, isn't he?"

Chapter 8

The first class of the first day of the fall semester: English literature. Already the seemingly ageless Miss Maude Sullivan was swaying in ecstasy as she quoted from Milton, giving the class a first-day taste of what was to come.

Behind her, as she stared out the window and spoke— more to herself than to the class, it seemed—the students settled into a variety of activities. Across the aisle from Terry, Madolyn Hollister scribbled furiously on a piece of notepaper. Probably she was writing a note to Bud Sherman. Certainly she was not making notes on Miss Sullivan's rambling appreciation of Milton's poetry. Up front, Kent

Westbrook was turned sideways in his seat, whispering to Brooke Shelton across the aisle. She was smiling at him. No remark about Milton's poetry had put the flirty smile on Brooke's face.

Other students, like Terry, sat rigidly at their desks, unmoving, staring straight ahead, their minds wandering away from the soft voice of Miss Sullivan. For sure, they were thinking about things other than Milton.

Terry's imagination told him that a pair of eyes was boring in on the back of his neck.

Thanks to Miss Sullivan's penchant for seating students in alphabetical order, Terry Masters was seated in front of Steve Palmer. Terry wished there had been a Murphy or a Norwood—somebody—to separate him from Steve.

Terry's dread of meeting Steve or any other of his former football teammates had only increased the longer he succeeded in avoiding them. He had heard from none of them during the ten days of preseason practice. And he had called none of them. He knew they were disappointed —probably even angry—with his decision to abandon football and so did not relish meeting them face to face. He told himself time and again that there was no hurry about facing up to them, that the encounter could wait. But no longer, not with classes starting.

In the shuffling that was involved in getting themselves in alphabetical order, Terry's and Steve's eyes had met.

Terry smiled and nodded. "How goes it?" he asked.

Steve did not return Terry's smile. "Fine," he said.

They were seated.

With his mind drifting away from the droning of Miss Sullivan, Terry wondered about the brief exchange with Steve. His friend and former teammate in the backfield of the Windsor High football team had been cool in his greeting. He still seemed angry and bitter. But was he? Terry reflected on the Steve Palmer he knew from the football team. Steve never had been a smiler or a back-slapper. He was serious, almost grim, most of the time. So maybe the unsmiling greeting meant nothing. Maybe the one word reply was not a rebuff. Terry frowned slightly. He was only vaguely aware of the sound of Miss Sullivan's voice. But he was sure he felt a pair of eyes boring into the back of his neck.

Finally the bell interrupted Miss Sullivan's monologue. She turned with a start, facing the class. Madolyn Hollister was looking up now, attentively watching the teacher. Kent Westbrook was still sideways in his seat, but the smile was gone and he was giving Miss Sullivan a thoughtful gaze. Brooke Shelton's flirty smile vanished in the instant it took Miss Sullivan to turn. She, too, stared at Miss Sullivan, an eyebrow raised as if to signify interest and alertness.

"Class dismissed," Miss Sullivan said.

Terry slid out of his seat, scooped up his books, and walked down the aisle. He sensed, rather than saw, Steve Palmer behind him and decided not to turn. He would not court friendship, even from an old teammate. Deliberately he walked down the aisle, determined not to rush away from Steve. Terry Masters was not in the habit of running away from anyone. If Steve wanted to extend himself, here was the chance. If Steve wanted to snub him— the word startled Terry; it seemed strange; nobody snubbed Terry Masters—well, if Steve wanted to try, here was the chance.

In the bottleneck at the door, Terry found himself side by side with Steve. Terry smiled slightly. The smile was automatic. With Terry, it was the instinctive smile of the star, used to acknowledging recognition by friends and strangers alike. Terry had learned the smile early in life. Steve, a star at quarterback, never had learned it. Steve met Terry's smile with a cold stare, and the smile faded.

If that's the way you want it, Terry thought, okay.

Outside the door, Steve and Terry both turned left, heading for the second class of the day. In the bustle of the corridor, jammed with students changing classes, Terry and Steve walked together. They had no choice for they were momentarily caught alongside each other.

"Man, I could not believe it," Steve said. Still unsmiling, he was looking at Terry. "Man, I still cannot believe it."

Terry sighed. He had already had his fill of talking about his abandonment of football, but he was relieved that Steve had spoken. The chilly greeting from Steve, whether only a natural part of Steve's personality or an intentional effort to snub, had bothered Terry. He did not

81

like the idea of the football players giving him the icy treatment.

"I could hardly believe it myself," Terry said.

"What do you mean?"

"Well, it had always been football with me, you know, ever since I was a small kid. I knew I wanted to change to soccer before I could admit it to myself. It came as kind of a surprise to me when I finally figured out what I wanted."

Steve was watching Terry. "I guess your dad blew his stack."

"Not bad."

"And Brundage?"

"Not bad. I was surprised."

"Did he tell you that you could come back if you changed your mind?"

Terry glanced quickly at Steve. He wondered what Wilson Brundage had told Steve of their conversation. Probably nothing. Terry knew full well that Wilson Brundage, like all the coaches Terry had dealt with, liked to keep a certain distance between himself and his players, even if the player happened to be his star quarterback. But Terry could almost hear Wilson Brundage's voice telling Steve: "He may decide to come back to football." And: "Let me know if you hear anything." Brundage was like that.

"He said to let him know if I changed my mind," Terry said slowly, wondering what was coming next from Steve.

But Steve said nothing.

"Who's running at left half—Ronnie Spurlock?"

Terry already knew the answer. He had read about the football team in the *Windsor Bulletin*. He had read the sportswriter's assessment of Spurlock's play, too: he was half a step slower than Terry Masters in making the turn on the sweeps around end. With Terry gone, a major weapon was removed from the Windsor Eagles' attack.

"Yeah, it's Ronnie."

"How's he doing?" He regretted the question the instant he asked it. He knew how Ronnie was doing. Not as well as Terry Masters, that's how. And he knew, too, that Steve was fully aware that Terry knew it. Ronnie had run second-string behind Terry last season. The question seemed to beg a compliment. Or, worse, seemed to force Steve to say Ronnie was doing a great job. "I mean—"

"We need Terry Masters as left half," Steve said flatly.

The statement embarrassed Terry. He wished more than ever that he had not asked how Ronnie was doing.

"I thought you would be back by now," Steve said. "I really did."

"Well, like I told you on sign-up day. . . ."

"I believed you then, but—"

"But what?"

"Well, that was before the Polish guy—what's his name?—showed up."

Terry felt himself flush. "What does he have to do with it?"

Steve was smiling slightly now. "Well, just that I hear he's pretty good."

Terry glared at Steve. Steve seemed to be enjoying the glare. "And, well, so what?" Terry asked.

"He was the big star in the first game, wasn't he?"

"He scored three goals," Terry said quickly. He thought immediately that the statement sounded silly, as if he were challenging Steve's statement. Terry was not used to being needled. But Steve had touched a nerve, and Terry had reacted as expected. He tried to recover. "Sure he was the star of the match," he said firmly.

"Well, that's what I mean," Steve said. Then, almost cheerily, he added, "Hey, this is where I go in—American history. See you later."

He veered away from Terry and disappeared through a door.

Terry walked on alone, frowning. A minute passed before he realized he had walked by his own classroom door, and he turned and retraced his steps.

Twice during the day teachers saw fit to comment as they looked over the new classes that Terry Masters had dropped football for soccer.

"I hear the football star has decided to become a soccer star this year," said Mrs. Stephens in the chemistry class. The reference to Terry as the star of the soccer team, in light of Krystian Wisniewski's performance in the opening game, caused Terry to blush. He was glad that Steve

Palmer was down the hall in another classroom. And he was glad that Bones Nelson, a senior, was not in the class. Mrs. Stephens smiled as she spoke, and the words had a friendly ring to them. But her pleasantness hardly helped.

With Owen Milliman, in European history, there was almost bubbly delight that Terry Masters was in his class. A tall, angular man, an institution at Windsor High for more than a decade, Milliman was a soccer buff. Three years ago he had taken an active roll in the push for a varsity soccer program at Windsor High. He appeared before the school board with his arguments that soccer was less expensive than football, safer for the players, and offered more opportunities for smaller boys to make the team. From the start of the first season, Owen Milliman had been the voice on the public-address system at the Eagles' home soccer matches.

"It's absolutely marvelous," he said, "seeing an athlete of your abilities choose to play soccer." Milliman was standing at the door, nodding to the students as they entered the classroom. "We are headed for a great season, don't you think?"

Terry smiled. "I hope so," he said. He expected Milliman to continue—"and how about that Krystian Wisniewski?"—but Milliman only smiled at Terry, saying nothing. Terry took a seat.

By the time he arrived at algebra class in the middle of the afternoon, Terry was relieved that the teacher was new to Windsor High. There was no risk that Mrs. Wainwright would offer another discomforting reminder that Terry Masters had stepped out of the spotlight. He had never seen Mrs. Wainwright before. She probably had never heard of Terry Masters, which was okay with him.

Terry walked into the classroom alone. Mrs. Wainwright, seated at her desk with the class roll in front of her, smiled pleasantly and nodded at Terry as he passed in front of her. Spotting Bob Traynor and Krystian seated at the far side of the room, Terry walked across and sat next to them.

"I'm going to like this course," Krystian said.

"Algebra?" Terry asked with a tone of amazement. The mathematics courses always gave him his greatest classroom difficulty.

Krystian grinned. "With mathematics, language is no problem," he said. "Numbers are numbers, whether Polish or English. Two plus two always equals four."

"Oh, yeah," Terry said, realizing for the first time the problems Krystian surely must have with American history or English literature, problems that would not bother students growing up in the United States.

"Well," said Mrs. Wainwright, getting to her feet behind the desk. "Welcome to second-year algebra." She smiled at the class. She nodded slightly toward the side of the room where Bob and Krystian and Terry were seated together. "I see that we have with us the new star of the soccer team."

Terry stared straight ahead.

Chapter 9

"The boys say that you want to come back to the football team."

Wilson Brundage spoke the words matter-of-factly, keeping his eyes on Terry seated across the desk. Brundage was frowning slightly, bringing his thick blond eyebrows together in a heavy line across his face.

This was the third day of school, Thursday, the day before the football team's opening game.

Terry was not surprised that the subject of the discussion was his possible return to the football team. He had known what Brundage wanted to talk about from the moment that Steve Palmer had said, "Coach wants to see you in his office, when you've got the time." Terry did not ask which coach. To Steve Palmer there was only one coach—Wilson Brundage. Terry did not ask why Brundage wanted to see him. He knew why. He had been expecting Brundage to make one last pitch at winning him back to the team. And now was the time.

The opening game of football season was one day away. After the first game, Terry knew, there would be no more invitations. Brundage would be committed to playing the season without Terry Masters. The other players had sweated and struggled through the preseason practice, earning their places on the team, while Terry had not been there. For purposes of team morale, if nothing else, the coach could not accept Terry after the first game had been played. Even now Brundage was courting trouble by opening the door for Terry. After the first game, the time for making special concessions would have passed. The players aside, Brundage had to think of the public eye. He could not appear to be needing—perhaps even begging for—Terry's return.

Terry understood. He was flattered, in a way, to see Brundage bending the rules even this much. But even more he felt a sense of relief. This interview was going to be the last of the pressure.

Yet Terry was puzzled by Brundage's opening statement. "The boys?" he asked.

Brundage continued to gaze at Terry, saying nothing.

88

Terry had said nothing to anyone—Steve or anyone else—about changing his mind. In his own mind, he knew without any doubts that the change to soccer was what he wanted. So it was impossible that he might have revealed, even unconsciously, a desire to go back to football.

Terry's mind raced back over the events of the last few days. Steve Palmer had said that he figured Terry would be back by now. He knew that Terry, used to being the star, was playing soccer in the shadow of Krystian Wisniewski. He was sure that Terry missed the spotlight and figured that Terry would run back to it—in football. He had told Terry as much in their brief conversation in the corridor. Had he told Brundage what he thought?

Or was Brundage merely using the term "the boys" as a ploy, to keep himself from appearing to be the one asking Terry to return? Maybe so.

Terry thought of his father. Perhaps his father had suggested that Brundage make one last try.

At first Terry felt anger—at Brundage, at Steve Palmer, at his father. They were trying to shove him away from something he wanted and into something he did not want. He wished they were off his back.

Then he felt a flush of embarrassment. They all knew that Terry Masters, who was used to being the star, was not the star of the soccer team. They all knew that a newcomer named Krystian Wisniewski had taken the spotlight. They all knew that Terry did not like it. They all—all of them?—had talked about it. Perhaps, they thought, Terry was disappointed with the way things were shaping up for him on the soccer team. Perhaps he regretted his decision now. Perhaps he was ready to change his mind. Terry imagined the thoughts of all of them—Brundage, Steve, his father—and he felt his face redden.

"You belong on the football team," Brundage said. The serious expression remained on his face. He watched Terry closely. "All of us—the boys and I—thought you would be back with us before now."

For a moment, Terry weighed the coach's remarks. In football, he was an all-conference performer. He was perhaps headed for selection on the all-state team, if not this year, then next year in his senior season. In soccer, he had had his moments of worry about winning a position in the starting lineup. He remembered the roaring cheers and the newspaper headlines he won as a football player. In soccer, few spectators showed up for the matches, and even fewer understood the game they were watching. But then Terry relived the sensational thrill of dribbling past an opponent, faking the goalie out of position, and booting home a goal.

"I told you in the first place, I'd rather play soccer," Terry said. He spoke slowly, his fists clenched. Consciously he opened his hands and tried to relax. He wanted desperately to get up and leave the office without another word. He wanted to be done with the interview. "And that's what I'm doing—playing soccer," he said.

Brundage leaned back in the chair and sighed.

"I like playing soccer better than playing football," Terry added.

Brundage's expression changed slightly. Terry recognized what was coming. He had seen the same expression on Steve Palmer's face when any sport other than football was mentioned. He had seen the expression on his father's face. It said: There is no sport but football.

Terry remembered the charge he had expected Brundage to level at him on sign-up day. He had not done so on that occasion, but he was going to now. Terry was sure of it. So he was not surprised when Brundage said, "Hitting never seemed to bother you before."

The last of Terry's embarrassment evaporated. He did not care whether Brundage had guessed that Terry missed the star's role before the excited, cheering crowds. He did not care either, if Wilson Brundage knew that the jarring collisions, the bone-rattling jolts of football did not add to the enjoyment of the game for Terry. He was tempted to say so. Brundage was trying to use a tactic that might work with some boys, but not with Terry.

With a conscious effort, Terry kept his gaze fixed on Brundage's eyes. He waited a moment, and then he spoke. "No," he said, "that's not it at all." He started to add, "And you know it." But he bit his lip instead and got to his feet. "Is that all?"

Brundage smiled slightly. "Wait a minute, Terry," he said.

Terry remained standing. He caught himself almost smiling at the coach's use of his first name. Does this mean I'm a man, Terry thought, or does it mean he thinks I never will be a man? He kept his eyes on the coach.

"Terry, this is the last chance," Brundage said. "You've already missed the preseason practice. As it is, I'm bending over backward for you. But we play our first game tomorrow night. After that"—he extended his hands, palms up— "there won't be a place for you on the team."

Terry nodded and turned toward the door. He had the door open when he turned back to Brundage. "Has my father spoken with you?" he asked.

Brundage shifted in his chair, and Terry was sure he knew the answer.

Terry stalked across the end of the gymnasium, frowning, hardly noticing the gym class engaged in a wild free-for-all of basketball.

"Hey, Masters—smile!" somebody shouted.

Terry walked on, into the hall and up the stairs and along the corridor, returning to his study hall. The anger surely showed in his face. Miss Milford blinked at him in surprise when she looked up casually to acknowledge his return. Terry hardly nodded at her, marching straight to his desk and sitting down. He stared straight ahead, his heart pounding. They would not quit trying to run his life for him.

When the bell rang ending the study period, Terry

gathered up his books and stepped outside into the corridor, where Steve Palmer was waiting for him. His face asked the question. Terry nodded briefly at Steve and walked past him without speaking.

Steve fell in step with Terry. "Did you see the coach?" he asked.

"I saw him," Terry said, staring straight ahead. He had no doubt that Steve knew in advance the subject of the interview. He might have even been the instigator. Who knew? "Yeah, I saw him," Terry repeated, continuing to walk along the corridor.

"And—"

"He said that I was afraid of the hitting."

"Wha-a-at?"

"You heard me."

"Well—"

Terry turned to Steve as they walk. "Well, what?" he snapped.

"Well, I—"

"Look," Terry said. "I've decided that I would rather play soccer, and I am playing soccer, and no amount of shoving by Coach Brundage or you—or anyone else—is going to change it. Understand?"

Steve's face clouded over. He stared at Terry for a moment. Then he said, "If that's the way it is."

"It is," Terry said, cutting away from Steve and turning into his classroom.

The last two classes of the day passed in a blur for Terry. He hoped he would not encounter Coach Brundage again, or Steve Palmer or any of the football players, before the final bell of the day. Fortunately, the Eagles were playing tonight. He was looking forward to the speed, the exertion, the competition—all of it—wiping away the events of the afternoon. At least nobody on the soccer team was trying to push him back into football.

Terry briefly considered telling Horst Schmidt about the visit with Coach Brundage, perhaps asking him to tell the football coach to lay off. But he decided against it. What difference did it make now? The matter was finished—not only the interview with Coach Brundage but the whole question of returning to the football team. Coach Brundage had laid down a deadline. Terry was letting it pass. That was that.

Except for his father.

Chapter 10

"Is anything wrong?"

Terry's father asked the question near the end of dinner that night. They were eating on the patio behind the house, the stone patio that Terry had helped his father lay the year before, seated at the heavy redwood table that Terry and his father had bolted together. The meal had been an unusually quiet one for the Masters dinner table. Terry was very much aware of his one-word answers—"fine," "okay," "sure"—to his parents' questions about the day's happenings. Terry's mother was aware of the abrupt answers too.

95

Terry could tell from the expression on her face, the slightly lifted eyebrow that asked a question without speaking. But she said nothing.

In his mind, Terry contrasted the stilted conversation of this evening with that of a year ago, the night before the first football game of the season. Together, Terry and his father had anticipated every play of the upcoming game, analyzed Terry's teammates, discussed the opponent. They argued strategy.

When Terry left football, he had realized that his father would not ask questions about the soccer team. His father did not know the questions to ask. They would not be able to discuss tactics or argue over strategy. Already Terry missed their comradeship over the football team. He missed, too, he had to admit, the unmistakable look of pride in his father's eye. Undoubtedly, his father missed these things also, and Terry couldn't help sharing his disappointment.

But tonight he repressed that feeling of disappointment time and again through the long, difficult dinner. He only felt anger at Wilson Brundage for trying to bully him back into football; he just kept seeing the expression on Brundage's face when Terry asked if the coach and his father had spoken.

Terry wished that the meal would end, that his mother would begin clearing away the dishes and his father would start packing away the barbecue utensils. Then he would tell him about the interview with Wilson Brundage and would tell him to lay off, quit meddling, forget about the change from football to soccer.

Before the moment arrived, however, Alvin Masters asked his question instead.

Terry's mother, as if on signal, stood and began collecting plates. "You two stay right there," she said. "I'll take care of these. But keep an eye on the time. What time is the match? Seven-thirty, isn't it?"

Terry mumbled, "Uh-huh."

His mother scooped up some plates and headed for the house. "It's almost six-thirty now," she said, as she walked away. She had sent her son off to enough athletic contests to know the need for time to change clothes and run through the warm-up drills. "You don't want to be late."

"I know," Terry said. He made a conscious effort to sound pleasant. Then he turned to his father.

"Is anything wrong?" his father asked again.

Words clattered through Terry's brain: lay off the pressure, get off my back, quit plotting with Wilson Brundage to get me to change my mind. But none of them came out.

His father leaned forward across the table. "Bluntly— just be blunt about it," he said.

"Okay," Terry said. He took a deep breath. "You've spoken with Coach Brundage?"

"When? Today?"

Terry nodded.

"No."

"No?"

"What are you talking about?" his father asked.

Terry hesitated. He was puzzled. He was sure the coach and his father had spoken. Brundage was certain to have called his father to report on the interview. After all, if they were scheming together, his father would have been awaiting the report. But his father was saying he had not spoken with Brundage. Would his father lie? Maybe, having learned from Brundage that the last-ditch effort failed, his father did not want Terry to know of his role. No, surely his father would not lie. But either way Terry's carefully crafted well-rehearsed indictment was in a shambles.

He plunged ahead anyway. "I don't appreciate your going behind my back to Wilson Brundage and trying to pressure me into going back to football."

His father frowned. "What in the world are you talking about?"

A brief warning flashed in Terry's mind. Something indeed was wrong here. Wilson Brundage had said—well, the same as said—that his father was a part of the one last pitch for him to return to football. Yet here was his father professing ignorance of the whole episode—and convincingly.

All the same, Terry found himself blurting out, "You've just got to understand that I like soccer better than football, and I'm going to play soccer instead of football, whether you like it or not." And, to his horror, more words escaped

98

him. "I'm sick of being the son of Alvin Masters on the football field."

His father blinked at Terry. Then, slowly, he picked up a fork and traced a light pattern, four little creases, in the bright green of the tablecloth.

Terry sat rigidly across from his father. He had gone too far. He knew it. He had probably hurt his father, perhaps unfairly, but that thought was crowded into the back of his mind by a chilling fear. He had revealed something that he had meant to keep entirely to himself.

"I see," his father said softly. The words came across to Terry as simply something to say, something to break the heavy silence between them. Then his father said, "Perhaps you should tell me what happened today."

There was no mention of being "the son of Alvin Masters on the football field."

Reciting the episode of the interview gave Terry a sense of relief. He began with Steve Palmer's first word that Brundage wanted to see him and ended with the final question to the football coach: "Has my father spoken with you?"

His father was watching Terry closely, waiting to hear what the football coach had answered.

"And he—" Terry stopped. "Then you didn't tell him to call me in for one last bit of pressure?" Terry said finally.

"No, I did not. And I would not.'

"I thought you had."

"I guess I can see how you might have thought that."

They sat for a moment without speaking. Terry wanted to look at his watch but didn't. He was going to be late for the match. By now his mother should have returned with a warning that he needed to get moving. But she didn't appear.

"I hope," his father said, "that you changed from football to soccer because you actually prefer playing soccer and not because you happen to be the son of Alvin Masters."

"I did," Terry said.

"I believe you," his father said. "When I saw you in the match last week, I knew that you were having more fun than you have ever had in any sport, football included."

Terry pursed his lips. He wanted to apologize for his remark but he was quiet.

His father broke the silence. "I've always known, Terry, that being the football-playing son of a football All-American was not easy."

"I shouldn't have made that crack," Terry said. "I was just—well, all the pressure and all."

"Yes, the pressure," his father said. "It's a word that you've used a lot this past week or so." He paused. "All of the pressure is not coming from the football side, is it? I mean, from Wilson Brundage and Steve Palmer and—I guess—from me too, is it?"

For an instant a kaleidoscope of scenes from the past

two weeks turned through Terry's mind. Horst Schmidt was looking at Krystian Wisniewski when he announced the arrival of important new talent on the team. The players were gawking in awe at Krystian—not Terry—in the first practice session. Bones Nelson was telling Hank that Terry could not stand being less than the star. Steve Palmer was grinning when he mentioned Krystian and the possibility of Terry returning to football, all in the same breath. His father, in the car riding home from the first match, was saying, "That Polish boy is one whale of a player, isn't he?"

"It'll work out," Terry said with a shrug.

"I'm sure it will," his father said.

They sat for a moment without speaking.

Then his father said, "Self-applied pressure is the toughest sort."

"Huh?"

His father smiled slightly. "Nobody can put pressure on you—not the coach, not your teammates, not the press, nobody—as hard as you can put it on yourself," he said. "And believe me, I know what I'm talking about."

"What do you mean?"

"You know, I didn't make the starting lineup as a sophomore."

Yes, Terry knew. He had heard the story all his life. Alvin Masters was an all-state halfback in high school. He was the star of his freshman team in college. That was back

101

in the days when frosh were not eligible for varsity play. Then as a sophomore, his first season on the varsity, Alvin Masters rode the bench as a second stringer. The next year, of course, he not only won the starting position but galloped his way to the All-American teams. Yes, Terry knew the story. He did not need to hear it again. Not now. He glanced at his watch.

"We've got a few minutes," his father said.

"Okay," Terry said. He slumped his shoulders slightly and fixed his eyes on a large elm tree beyond his father.

"Talk about pressure," Alvin Masters said. "I never felt it in a game the way I felt it on the sidelines, a second stringer. I could imagine what the people back home were saying. I was sure that I knew what my teammates were thinking: the hotshot is riding the bench. Sometimes at games I thought I could hear conversations from the fans in the grandstand."

Terry shifted his gaze from the elm tree to his father. He had not heard this side of the story before.

"I got myself so uptight that when I did finally get into a game—it was the second game of the season—I fumbled the handoff the first time I got the ball."

"I didn't know that," Terry said.

His father smiled. "It was horrible."

"I guess."

"Walking off the field after that fumble, I decided to quit football."

"Really?"

"Really. I was going to keep walking, all the way to the dressing room, and then leave and never come back." He paused. "But I didn't, because I always have loved the game, and I still do." He paused again. "Pretty quickly after that horrible day I began to learn a couple of things. For one, the player who was starting ahead of me in the lineup was pretty good. He deserved to be where he was. But more important, I figured out that I was the only one applying pressure to Alvin Masters. Nobody else thought it was a disaster that I was a second stringer as a sophomore. My family and the other people back home were proud that I was playing at all. That came as a surprise when I was home for the Christmas break. And my teammates didn't consider the second string a disgrace for a sophomore. Some of them were second stringers as seniors. The people in the grandstands weren't mumbling to themselves in shock about Alvin Masters riding the bench."

Terry's mother appeared in the back door. She slid open the glass panel. "Do you know what time it is?" she asked.

"We're on our way," Terry's father called back to her. Then he turned back to Terry. "The pressure had been bothering me, keeping me from playing my best, and I was the only one applying it. So I quit."

Chapter 11

Terry was late arriving at the field for the Eagles' match with the Fox Valley Raiders. His father let him out of the car at the gate to the field and drove away alone to locate a parking place. Terry stepped through the gate and jogged across the end of the field toward the door to the gymnasium.

His father's words—"I was the only one applying the pressure"—remained in his mind. Terry got the point. Sometimes you have to settle for less than being the brightest star on the field. Sometimes you have to do without the cheers. There is no reason to be ashamed. And if you have enough love of the game, and enough playing ability, perhaps stardom will come with hard work. In the case of Alvin Masters, it had. But either way don't fret, don't worry—don't apply pressure. Terry understood.

As he jogged under the football goalposts, Terry glanced up at the bleachers on the west side of the field. He was surprised by the size of the crowd. Already there were more than twice the number of people who had turned out for the Eagles' opening match a week ago.

Terry smiled slightly. The Eagles' overwhelming victory —by a score of 9–0 in the opening match—had stirred up enthusiasm. Terry remembered the electric feeling of the match's opening moments, the sensation of triumph, the thrill of certain victory. Every player on the team had sensed it before the match was a minute old, and the knowledge showed in every movement on the field. As always, the aura of victory, when evident among the players on the field, was quick to spread to the fans in the bleachers and beyond, to the people who hear about the team and will not miss the next match. The proof was in the crowd here tonight.

Then Terry's smile faded. He had to admit to himself, "The word about Krystian Wisniewski has spread quickly." He glanced up at the crowd. They've come out to see the new Polish guy—what's his name?—that everybody is talking about.

By the time Terry reached the door to the gym he was

frowning. He decided that his father's story about self-imposed pressures did not help a bit. Terry Masters did not like being in the shadows, watching someone else perform in the spotlight. A parable from his father's football-playing days was not going to change that. He was frowning, too, because of the very telling of the tale. His father had picked up on his word *pressure* and had read Terry's frustrations. Terry did not find the thought comfortable.

Inside the gymnasium, Terry took the steps leading down to the locker room two at a time and pushed his way through the swinging door.

Bones Nelson, already in uniform, was tieing a shoe. He looked up. He seemed surprised to see Terry.

"I'm late," Terry said to no one in particular. "Couldn't help it."

Horst Schmidt gave Terry a stern look. The coach did not like tardiness, at practice or at a match. He did not ask Terry for an explanation. There was none he would accept.

"Hurry up and change, Terry," Schmidt said.

The other players were suited out, almost ready to take the field for the warm-up drills. They all, to the last player, were giving Terry strange looks, ranging from the surprise on Bones's face to questioning glances.

Terry felt like saying, "Is it such a sin to be a few minutes late? I'm here, aren't I? I'll be ready for the match." But he nodded to the coach without speaking and started unbuttoning his shirt as he walked to his locker.

"Where have you been?" asked Hank Dodsworth. He was wearing his red-and-white striped goalie's shirt, ready to leave the locker room for the field. He spoke softly, standing next to Terry at the locker. A few players already were drifting out the door toward the field. "Everybody was wondering."

"Wondering what?" Terry spoke curtly. He was in no mood for probing questions or accusations. His anger from the interview with Wilson Brundage was still there. His father's remarks, intended to be helpful, had been troublesome instead. Then, jogging across the field, he had been reminded of Krystian Wisniewski by the surprisingly large crowd in the bleachers. And now, walking into the locker room, he encountered a ring of surprised and questioning faces. He did not need Hank's questions. "I've had a busy day," Terry said, and concentrated on removing his street clothes.

"What'd Brundage want?"

"Huh?" Terry turned his head to look at Hank. "Where did you hear about that?"

"It's all over the place that he called you in for a meeting."

Terry glanced past Hank at the few remaining players putting on their uniforms and tieing their shoes. They were paying no attention to him now. But Hank's statement explained Bones's startled expression and the odd looks of the others when he walked in late.

At the far end of the dressing room, Terry saw Horst Schmidt talking with Krystian against the wall. He wondered if Schmidt knew. If so, Schmidt must have read his own answers into the questions about Terry's tardiness. Maybe Schmidt did not know. Maybe it was just student chatter.

"Brundage wanted to know if I'd changed my mind."

"And—"

"And I'm here, aren't I?"

"Yeah," Hank said. He spoke slowly, uncertainly, as if another question remained in his mind, unspoken but demanding an answer.

"Look," Terry said, understanding the question in Hank's mind. "I wasn't late tonight because of that. I wasn't sitting around out there somewhere trying to make up my mind, if that's what you're thinking."

"Okay," Hank said, with a sheepish grin.

"I got involved in a conversation with my father at dinner. It ran longer than it should've. That's all."

"Okay, okay," Hank said. He didn't have to ask the topic of conversation at the Masters family dinner table. Everyone in Windsor knew that Alvin Masters dreamed of another Masters being named to the All-American football teams. The dream was evident to everyone, and Hank knew even better than most. "How's your father taking it?"

"He's okay."

Horst Schmidt's heavily accented voice stopped the conversation. "Hank, let's go," he called out. "And you, Terry, get a move on. C'mon."

Schmidt barked the words as he walked out of the dressing room, headed for the field.

Hank turned and fell into line behind Schmidt and Jorge Perez and Henrik Sterner.

"Right with you," Terry called out.

Henrik, with the rest of them already out the door, leaned back in. "Yeah, Masters, get a move on!" he snapped in mock severity. Then, laughing, he ducked out the door before Terry could turn.

Terry pulled on his shirt, quickly tied his shoes, and followed the team onto the field in a run for the warm-up drills. The giant arc lights bathed the field in brightness. The evening was warm, dry, windless—perfect for soccer.

The crowd was indeed more than twice the size of the turnout at the opening match a week earlier. At a glance, Terry could not spot his father among the spectators scattered through the bleacher seats on the west side of the field. The bleachers on the east side were closed, with one guard sitting alone, keeping any wandering spectators from settling in. If the east bleachers were not needed, there was one set of bleachers less to clean up for the football game the next night, when both bleachers would be packed to capacity.

Terry jogged under the football goalposts, circled around the soccer goal, and easily picked up a dribble with a loose

109

ball. He turned and drilled a shot toward the goal. It went wide.

He turned back. At the other end of the field he could see the Fox Valley Raiders, wearing their purple-and-silver uniforms, racing through their warm-up drills. The Raiders had won their opening match the week before by a 3–1 score. As Terry watched them, he remembered Horst Schmidt's words at the close of practice the day before: "The Raiders are better—much better—than the Henderson Park Panthers, and you'd better believe it."

Terry understood the coach's message: Don't be overconfident. But neither he nor any of the other players gave the coach's warning more than a shrug.

Having won their opening match 9–0, the Eagles had rollicked through the practice sessions. Krystian Wisniewski, with the quickness of a hare and the grace of a ballet dancer, was unstoppable. Bones Nelson was unerring at forward. Henrik Sterner at sweeper and Hank Dodsworth behind him were surely impenetrable on defense. Terry was strong at forward and deadly with the header shots coming off Krystian's corner kicks. So what was there to worry about?

Terry wove back into the dribbling drill. Whistles blew, and Terry and the other Eagles ran to the sideline for the last moment before the start of the match.

Horst Schmidt listed the starting lineup—no changes from the opening match the week before—while the referee circled the group, checking cleats.

110

"Don't take these fellows lightly," Schmidt said. "You must work, and you must concentrate. Anything less—if you go out there and play around—you will be in for a surprise. They will beat you."

Terry had heard coaches say the same thing before—in football, baseball, basketball. They always seemed to say it just before what turned out to be an overwhelming victory. He could not remember playing in a losing match after getting the standard overconfidence warning.

Glancing at the faces around him in the group at the sideline, Terry could see that not a one of them believed they were in the slightest danger of losing. And in the end they weren't.

Krystian pounded home two goals, both on spectacular long dribbles. Bones got one goal on a short shot from his center forward position in front of the nets. Terry scored one goal, kicking into the corner of the nets after faking the goalie the other way. The Eagles defeated the Fox Valley Raiders by a score of 4–1.

"Wiz the Whiz!" shouted Bones in the dressing room.

Everyone cheered. Nobody shouted, "Terry the Whiz!"

Chapter 12

The cheers for Krystian in the dressing room lasted for only a few minutes.

Still, Terry could not help resenting them.

Quickly he showered, dressed, and headed for the door alone.

Suddenly Hank Dodsworth materialized alongside him. Terry did not feel like company. He especially did not feel like having the company of his best friend. A stranger would have been easier to take. But there was no shaking loose from Hank. They lived in the same direction from the school building, and, it being a school night, both were headed straight home.

"Nice game," Hank said. "You played well."

They were walking around the side of the school building toward the sidewalk in front. The outside lights of the building and the streetlights cast funny shadows in the darkness of the summer night.

"Thanks," Terry said, staring straight ahead.

They walked in silence for a moment. Then Hank said, "You're missing being the star of the team."

Terry took a deep breath but said nothing.

"Maybe Bones was right," Hank said.

"What does Bones know? He's just jealous."

Hank said nothing, seeming to weigh his words, trying to decide whether to speak at all. "Bones knows—we all know —and you know, too, that when you signed up for the soccer team, you looked like a cinch to be the best player on the team. You're a better player than Bones. Nobody else was even close to being as good as you are. But then, all of a sudden, there was Krystian."

"What's wrong with wanting to be the best?"

"There's a difference between being the best and being the star."

Terry looked at Hank. "Oh?"

"You ought to play goalie sometime. I'm a good goalie. I think I'm one of the best goalies in the conference. But who cheers the goalie? It's like playing defensive tackle on a football team. You have to be good or the team is in trouble. But nobody cheers for you."

"You don't understand."

Hank did not reply for a moment. They walked along the darkened street in silence. Then he said, "You're hurting yourself, and you're going to hurt the team."

"Hurting? I scored a goal tonight."

"Yeah, I know," Hank said. "But you're not going to be playing your best if all you're thinking about is being the star. And it's not going to help the team if everybody thinks that all you're interested in is being the star."

"I thought you were my friend."

"Don't get mad."

"I'm not mad."

"I am your friend, and that's why I'm talking to you."

Terry took a deep breath. Hank's argument seemed somehow to have a vague resemblance to his father's story, only a few hours earlier. His father had worried about what people were thinking. He built up so much pressure on himself that he fumbled when he finally got into a game. But he loved football, and he stuck it out. Terry loved soccer. He wanted to play soccer. Did he want it enough to settle for being less than star of the team? He always had been the star. He liked it. People expected it of him. What were people thinking?

Hank broke the moment's silence. "It shows," he said.

"What?"

"I said, it shows."

Terry did not speak. He did not have to ask what Hank meant. He had known from the start. Bones Nelson had been right. He realized that Terry expected, and with good reason, to win the spotlight in soccer. Then Bones learned of Krystian Wisniewski. He had predicted that Terry would not easily swallow being eclipsed by someone else. And now Hank was saying that everybody—maybe even Horst Schmidt—was seeing Bones's forecast come true.

"Okay," Terry said. "I see your point."

By the time Terry arrived for the football game on Friday night, the bleachers on both sides of the field were almost filled. The sounds and sights of the scene were comfortably familiar to Terry—the noise of the crowd, the blaring of the band, the arc lights bathing the field in a shadowless bright-ness, the excitement of the final moments before the opening kickoff of the season.

Turning the corner of the bleachers, he stopped and gazed at the scene. He expected to feel again the wave of nostalgia for the game he had left behind. He expected to find himself wishing—well, at least half wishing—that he was among the players in the dressing room getting their last-minute instructions from Wilson Brundage. But to his surprise he felt no homesickness for football.

"I'm a soccer player now," he told himself, and there was relief in the thought.

At the moment, his role in the shadows, watching the spotlight play on Krystian Wisniewski, did not matter. Terry's main concern was finding his seat, and he scanned the crowded bleachers quickly.

Somebody shouted, "Hey, Terry-baby, they're going to miss you out there tonight."

Terry smiled and waved in the direction of the shout. No matter what Hank had said, and no matter what his father had said, and no matter how right they might be, it was nice to be known.

Terry was searching the crowd for Hank or Henrik or Krystian. He had agreed to join Hank and Henrik in the introduction of the Polish boy to football, American style. The idea was Hank's, and Terry liked it, for it would help him prove to the world—and to himself—that he felt no jealousy. Terry spotted Henrik waving at him from halfway up the bleachers. Krystian was seated next to him. Terry waved back and moved up the steps toward them.

"Hey, look who's here! It's Masters!" somebody shouted. Somebody else shouted, "Hey, Terry!"

Terry grinned and waved as he moved up the bleacher steps through the crowd.

"Hey," Terry said, sliding into a seat between Henrik and Krystian that they had saved for him, "where's Hank?"

"Not here yet," Henrik said absently. He was waving at someone in the crowd.

"The fans recognize you," Krystian said. "I heard them calling out to you."

116

"Yeah," Terry said. He shoved the hair back off his forehead and stared at the empty football field before him.

"Terry was the star of the football team last year," Henrik said.

"Is that it?" Krystian asked. "They recognize you from the football team? I thought they recognized you from the soccer team."

"Nah," Henrik said. "The football fans remember him from last year. He was the star."

Terry glanced at Henrik. The remark pricked like a needle. But Henrik was looking away, scanning the crowd for familiar faces.

"Do you miss it?" Krystian asked.

Terry wondered for a brief moment if Krystian were asking whether Terry missed playing football or missed being the star of the team. Krystian's pleasant smile offered no answer for Terry.

"I like soccer better," Terry said.

"There's Hank now," Henrik said. He stood and waved.

Hank waved back and began climbing the steps. He dropped into the aisle seat Henrik had been saving. "I thought I was going to miss the kickoff," he said.

"Almost did," Henrik replied. "Here they come now."

The Eagles came onto the field, prancing single file through the corridor of cheerleaders. The fans in the bleachers on both sides of the field got to their feet with a roaring cheer. Terry stood, too, clapping his hands.

From the other end, the Dunton Heights Trojans took

the field. A roar went up from the small crowd of Dunton Heights fans who had driven in for the game.

At the Eagles' bench, the players crowded around the familiar figure of Wilson Brundage. The players were jumping and slapping each other on the shoulder pads. Terry could almost feel the old excitement, nervousness, anticipation of combat. Brundage was saying something. Terry could see the coach's mouth working. But as he knew, even the players closest to the coach could not hear everything he was saying above the din of the players, the crowd, and the band.

The fans stood through the coin flip and the kickoff and then settled into their seats to watch the game.

On the second play from scrimmage, Steve Palmer pitched out to Ronnie Spurlock. The play was a patented Terry Masters gainer for the Eagles last season: an end sweep with the halfback gathering in the ball on the dead run and turning on the speed upfield. Terry found himself clenching his fists. Ronnie, slow in making the turn, got knocked down for no gain.

A long, low moaning sound—"Ooooooh"—swept through the bleachers. Ronnie Spurlock was, as the sportswriter had described him, a half step too slow.

Terry, chin on his hand, watched the Eagles return to the huddle and waited for somebody to shout, "Hey, Terry, you'd have gone all the way with that one." But no one did.

By half time the Eagles were leading 14–7, thanks to

Steve Palmer's accurate passing and the fact that the Eagles gave up trying to send Ronnie Spurlock racing around the ends.

When the players trooped off the field toward the dressing room for the intermission, Terry and the three others stood and joined the slow, shuffling movement of the crowd toward the refreshment stand.

Terry got a Coke and, turning, spotted his father talking to a tall, bald-headed man wearing wire-rim glasses. With or without Terry Masters in the lineup, Alvin Masters was not about to miss a Windsor Eagles' football game.

His father stepped over toward Terry. "Not so good, huh?" he said. "Ought to be more than 14–7. This Dunton Heights team isn't that strong."

"Uh-huh," Terry said. He waited for his father to say, "They're missing you out there at halfback."

But instead he said, "Well, they'll pull it out."

Henrik, Hank, and Krystian gathered around, sipping their Cokes.

Terry's father greeted Hank. "How's the world's greatest goalie?"

Hank looked around with feigned puzzlement. "Is he here tonight too?" Everyone laughed.

Terry introduced his father to Henrik and Krystian.

"I've seen your matches," Mr. Masters told them. "You're loaded with talent, and"—he nodded toward Krystian—"with this young man in there, you're really loaded."

Krystian smiled. "Thank you," he said softly.

Terry eyed Krystian. He thought of Hank's words: "It shows." He wondered if Krystian sensed—or knew—of his disappointment. Probably so. But Krystian, always so cool, so aloof, never offered the slightest hint. Perhaps he simply did not care. He was good enough to be above it all, and he knew it.

The four boys moved through the crowd toward the bleachers. The teams were coming back on the field for the second half.

Sliding into their seats, Terry heard someone shout, "Wiz the Whiz!" The voice was Bones Nelson's. Terry and the others looked down at the rows in front of them. There was Bones, standing at his seat, grinning and waving. "Wiz the Whiz at his first football game," Bones shouted.

Krystian waved back.

With an effort, Terry waved too.

As they sat down, a man in front and to the right of Terry turned and stared at Krystian for a moment.

The man next to him said, "What'd he say—Wiz the Whiz?"

"Yeah, it's the Polish boy—what's his name—on the soccer team. You've heard about him, haven't you?"

The man turned and looked at Krystian. "Wiz the Whiz," he repeated. "Yeah, I heard something."

Terry stared straight ahead. He was sure all four of them had heard the conversation. He could feel Hank's eyes on him. He wondered what Krystian was thinking. He remembered Krystian's question—"Do you miss it?"—about football, or was the question about being the star of the team?

"It won't show," Terry told himself over and over.

On the field, the teams were lining up for the kickoff that started the second half.

Chapter 13

The name stuck—Wiz the Whiz. Krystian seemed amused, flattered—and puzzled. "I looked it up in the dictionary," he said in his heavily accented English one day before practice. "And *whiz* means a hissing sound."

Everyone in the dressing room roared with laughter. Even Horst Schmidt, who seldom smiled when the serious business of soccer was at hand, broke into a grin.

Terry, too, could not help laughing. In the days since his talk with Hank, Terry had laughed when he had not felt like it. He had cheered when he did not feel like cheering. Hank's "It shows" lodged in his mind. He was determined that his disappointment would *not* show. But this time he laughed genuinely. The confused expression on the face of Wiz the Whiz made the remark seem all the funnier.

Bones Nelson tried to explain to Krystian that he was not being labeled a hissing sound. "If you're a whiz, well, you're a whiz—and that's good," he said.

"It's slang," Hank chimed in.

Krystian shrugged and smiled.

The nickname was there to stay.

The Eagles' winning ways seemed there to stay too. With Wiz leading the way, the Eagles marched past their next six opponents in a breeze. None of the opponents even came close to knocking them off. The Eagles found themselves approaching the halfway mark of their schedule at the end of September—undefeated, untied, and virtually unchallenged in eight straight matches.

All the way, Wiz dominated the field. His dribbling and passing on offense and his deft tackling and fearsome dueling on defense wiped out the opponents. His scoring ability on forays to the goal mouth not only piled on points for the Eagles, it helped Terry and Bones and Archie become more effective forwards. Edgy defenders trying to keep track of Wiz left the forwards open for their own shots on goal. Terry knew he prospered in the shadow of Wiz's abilities, scoring goals while a frustrated defense was keeping one eye on the slender Polish boy who seemed to be everywhere at the same time.

To be sure, all of them—Terry and Bones and Archie

123

up front, the flanker halfbacks, the fullbacks, the sweeper, the goalie—contributed to the awesome success of the Eagles. But one player stood out as the key to all the victories: Krystian Wisniewski, Wiz the Whiz.

Wiz was the hub of the attack, the essential element in every offensive play Horst Schmidt introduced. If not the shooter, Wiz was the passer who set up a teammate's goal. Or he was the decoy who drew the defenders' attention to himself, freeing a teammate for a shot on goal.

Helping to build the attack around another player was a new experience for Terry, who was used to being the hub himself. He could not help feeling resentment. Occasionally he caught himself glancing around at his teammates for some sign of resentment on their part. It must be there. Having felt his teammates' resentment in football and basketball when coaches laid out plays guaranteed to make him a star, Terry was now learning how it felt to be on the other end. But he found no allies on the soccer team. The Eagles were winning and loving every minute of it. And all of the Eagles owed a large share of their individual success to the Polish player with the quick feet and the unfailing instinct for the ball. Wiz was making them all look good. Terry acknowledged the fact, but he could not bring himself to relish the thought.

At the end of the first eight matches, Wiz led the Eagles in scoring with fourteen goals. Terry was second with eleven—three of them, he grudgingly admitted to himself,

124

on headers resulting from Wiz's skill with corner kicks, always placing the ball precisely where Terry needed it for a header into the goal. Bones was third in scoring with eight goals—already two thirds of his total goal production of twelve the previous season.

Conversely, Wiz owed virtually nothing of his stardom to Terry. Seldom was a Terry Masters pass the reason for a goal by Wiz. Even when it happened, Wiz's skill with the approach and the shot outshined the assist. When he was honest with himself, Terry could not remember a single instance when the threat of his presence at the goal mouth freed Wiz for a shot.

Wiz took it all with a smile and a shrug, cool acceptance with a touch of modesty, a technique Terry recognized with a pang as one of his own when he had been on the football field.

Terry tried to tell himself that starring was not important. He loved playing soccer, and that was what mattered, not who was the star. Terry repeated the statement to himself over and over again.

Yet Terry missed the spotlight. At the matches and in the corridors of the school, the name Terry heard was not his own. It was Wiz the Whiz. But Hank's words—"It shows"—never left Terry's mind. He was determined to keep his feelings to himself, a guarded secret. So he was always the first to pat Wiz on the back after a goal. He always gave Bones his biggest hug after a goal. His shouts of congratulation to teammates making a good play were the loudest of all.

Now, after the eighth match, Terry thought he was pulling it off. Hank had said nothing more, which Terry figured was a good sign. Even Bones Nelson seemed to be changing his mind. No more did Terry catch Bones eyeing him suspiciously. No more did Bones ring out with the shout "Wiz the Whiz" every time Terry was in earshot and then turn on that crooked little grin. Maybe somebody, perhaps Hank, had told Bones to lay off. But either way Terry had the feeling that he was convincing Hank and Bones and all the rest of them that they had been mistaken.

The spectacular success of the Eagles, plus the spreading word about Wiz the Whiz, doubled and redoubled the size of the crowds attending the matches. The small knots of people who had attended the first match, families and friends of the players, were swallowed up in the crowds turning out now.

By the fourth match, the cheerleaders were out in force too, all ten of them. No longer was a Windsor High soccer match the province of the three cheerleaders who had volunteered in the preseason to show up each Tuesday and Thursday night to provide token support for the boys playing the strange new game.

By the sixth match, the school officials had to open up the bleachers on the east side of the field to accommodate the crowds who turned out to cheer them on. They were

126

learning the game, thanks to the flickering feet and dazzling passes of Wiz the Whiz.

The winning fever caught the players, too. No longer did they amble onto the field from the dressing room. No longer did they move casually into their warm-up drills. They ran onto the field, looking for all the world like an unstoppable force. They raced by their bench, picking off soccer balls from the cluster on the ground, and zipped onto the field. After all, they were the undefeated Windsor High Eagles.

In the moment before the start of a match, they clasped hands in front of the bench, leaping and shouting, a ritual that Horst Schmidt seemed to view with some distaste. To him, soccer was a game of skill, not emotion. But he never said anything to deter his players from their whooping cheer before taking the field.

For Terry, those moments just before a match and the thrilling minutes of play on the field were a world apart from the frustrations of his new role. The anticipation of the competition, the competition itself, the thrill of being winners—these things overrode the gnawing absence of individual stardom for himself.

If the skyrocketing fortunes of the Eagles affected Horst Schmidt in the slightest, he never let it show. All business and unsmiling, he moved his Eagles methodically from match to match. He drilled the players the same way. He pounded away at the fundamentals—dribbling, tackling, shooting on goal. And he always, always inserted a new little wrinkle of some sort in the attack, giving each opponent something unexpected.

After each victory he made the same statement to the players in the dressing room: "You played well tonight, and you deserved to win, but this was not the best team you will face this season."

Then came the Linden Tigers.

Chapter 14

"I have been telling you that the teams you defeated were not the best teams you will face this season," Horst Schmidt said. "Tonight is different."

The coach was standing in the middle of the dressing room. He was wearing his soccer field uniform—khaki trousers, gray sweatshirt, blue baseball cap, and soccer shoes. His face was serious. His words were spoken softly.

Around him, the players sat on the benches in front of their lockers, except for Bones Nelson. Bones stood with his arms folded tightly over his chest, repeatedly shifting his weight from one foot to the other. That was okay. In the case of Bones Nelson, the jumpier he was the better. Bones's nervousness translated into action on the playing field. Everyone knew it.

Terry sat slouched back, leaning against the door of his locker, his hands folded across his stomach, legs stretched out in front of him. Inside, his heart was pounding furiously. But he wore a sober expression, outwardly calm. He had long ago mastered the technique of masking his nervousness behind a facade of relaxed composure. He had played in big matches before, in football, baseball, basketball. This was no different. He raised a hand to push his hair back off his forehead, keeping his eyes on the coach. The hair flopped back down.

Outside, the night was chilly but dry and windless. It was perfect weather for a soccer match. The ground passes, unencumbered by moisture, would skitter over the grass with dazzling speed. The long kicks, with neither the help nor the hindrance of the wind, would find their targets with all the accuracy the kicker could deliver. Nature was offering no advantages or disadvantages to either team this night.

"You must mark your men tonight tighter than ever before," Horst Schmidt said. "A slip, one slip, a moment's opening in front of the goal, and the Linden Tigers will score."

Terry was barely listening. He knew about the Linden Tigers. He had read the stories in the newspaper. The Linden Tigers, like the Eagles, were undefeated, having

130

rolled over eight opponents straight, all by overwhelming scores. With a soccer program three years older than the program at Windsor High, the Tigers had the Eagles whipped in depth and experience. Besides, the Tigers were blessed with the presence of two Mexican boys, lifelong soccer players, at halfback. Both of them, Adolpho Camacho and Miguel Toledano, were of Wiz's caliber—fancy dribblers, expert passers, tough duelers, deadly when shooting on goal.

As he spoke, Coach Schmidt was looking at the back line players of the Eagles. The Eagles' defenders were in for a battering at the hands of the explosive Linden Tigers. Hank Dodsworth, whose goalkeeper position was the last line of defense for the Eagles, sat leaning forward, elbows on his knees, taking his breath in huge gulps. The others in the defense—the sweeper, Henrik Sterner, and the fullbacks, Woody Clark, Chuck Horton, and Bob Traynor—returned the coach's gaze from their positions on the benches. Henrik was nodding slightly as the coach spoke. There were no wisecracks from Henrik tonight.

"On the attack, you must shoot, shoot, shoot, and shoot again," Coach Schmidt said. "Keep the pressure on—and keep it on *at the goal*. Don't get yourself boxed into dribbling down the touchline. It looks pretty, but it scores no goals. Keep centering. Keep shooting. We must bombard them with shots on goal."

To take advantage of the dry field and the windless night, Schmidt outlined a strategy of long kicks—a rare

131

strategy for a Horst Schmidt team—to keep placing the ball in the Linden end of the field, at the mouth of the Linden goal.

"Our match tonight does not call for fancy footwork at midfield when we are attacking," he said. "Against those two Mexican boys at halfback, you won't get away with it. Our strategy tonight is *not*—repeat: *not*—to try to play ball-control soccer. The only ball control that we want tonight is keeping the ball at the Linden goal mouth—and in the Linden goal. Keep centering, and put the ball where we can shoot on goal, and then shoot, shoot, shoot."

The coach paused and let the words sink in. He glanced around the room at the players.

Terry straightened himself in his seat on the bench. He nodded slightly when Schmidt's glance passed over him. He pushed his hair back off his forehead again.

Horst Schmidt's words confirmed what Terry had figured out for himself on the practice field the day before. For Terry Masters, the match with the Linden Tigers was more than a major collision of two unbeaten soccer teams. Sure, the match was going to be one of the toughest tests—and one of the most important—of the season for the Windsor Eagles. Probably the match was a battle for the conference championship. In itself, the importance of the match was enough to get Terry's heart pounding. But tonight there was more than the excitement of a big match quickening Terry's heartbeat. Clearly, the match tonight belonged to the forwards—Terry, Bones, and Archie—and not to Wiz the Whiz. The strategy that was required to overcome the Linden Tigers left no choice.

Horst Schmidt had stopped short of saying so, but Wiz, for all his skills, was sure to have more than his hands full trying to cope with the dazzling play of the two Mexican boys on the Linden team. The unspoken acknowledgment had become obvious in the shape and form of the drills on the practice field the day before. The point of the Eagles' strategy was to try to minimize the burden on Wiz at midfield and try to carry the battle away from the skillful Mexican boys to the mouth of the Linden goal.

Now the coach had, in effect, put Terry's conclusions into words: long kicks to the goal mouth and—shoot, shoot, shoot.

Surely, if the Eagles were to win the match, Wiz must turn in an outstanding game dueling with the Mexican boys at midfield, but it was clear to Terry that this was not a match when Wiz, with his quick moves, sure dribbling, and accurate passing would be the brightest star on the field. The Mexican boys surely knew about Wiz. They would be trying to keep the ball away from him when the Tigers were on the attack. They would be with Wiz, step for step, when he raced forward to join the Eagles on the attack.

Certainly he was not going to be overpowering anyone at midfield or outplaying them on the attack in this match. This time Wiz's assignment was to hold his own. He could be asked to do no more.

Victory for the Eagles rested with the others—the for-

133

wards for the scoring punch, the other two halfbacks to help Wiz in his task at midfield, the back line to stop the Tigers without their usual help from Wiz.

The thought struck Terry, and surprised him, that against the Linden Tigers, the Eagles on the field were—for the first time—more than the supporting cast for Wiz. More than any other match, this one required all-out team effort.

Wiz was sitting next to Terry with his knees up, hugging them, watching the coach. If Wiz feared for his ability to meet the test, he did not show it. If he saw himself fated by the strategy to fade back into the shadows, he gave no indication that it mattered.

Terry glanced at Archie McAlister, sitting on a bench across from him. Archie was sitting slightly forward, his hands gripping his thighs. He repeatedly dug his thumbs into the inside of his thighs. Archie was nervous. Of the three forwards, Archie was the weak link. If the match belonged to the forwards, it was to be shared by Terry and Bones.

Terry looked to his left at Bones, standing against the wall and rubbing his hands together as if drying them. Funny, Terry thought, how Archie's nervousness was a weakness and Bones's nervousness was a strength, energy ready to be unleashed. Terry knew that his own well-disguised nervousness was a good sign. He always played best when the adrenalin flowed. He was ready tonight.

Bones quit rubbing his hands and locked his arms across his chest again, all the while jerkily shifting his weight from one foot to another. His eyes met Terry's for a moment. Terry looked away.

In the momentary quiet of the dressing room, Terry could hear the crowd from outside. The cheerleaders were taking the fans through one of the Eagles' rhythmic cheers, ending with a screeching shriek, the cry of an eagle. For this match, the bleachers on both sides of the field were nearly filled, and the cheers were clearly audible in the dressing room.

"All right, let's go," Horst Schmidt said.

Terry stood up. He took a deep breath.

"Trailer left!"

Terry heard the shout from behind in the broken English of Wiz.

The match was ten minutes old and still scoreless.

Terry, having won a duel at the touchline, was dribbling at an angle toward the Linden goal, heading into a crowd of defenders.

The running duel at the touchline had brought the fans in the bleachers to their feet. Terry's triumph in the duel—the theft of the ball from the Linden halfback—had brought a roar of approval from the crowd. Perhaps Terry Masters's victory in the duel would set up the first goal of the match, putting the Eagles out front. Terry, whirling away from the defeated Linden halfback, was thinking one word: goal.

Terry knew the meaning of Wiz's shouted signal. He was twenty yards out from the goal. The defenders were closing in. Terry appeared to be at the end of the line. He was sure to be stopped and bottled up, perhaps to lose the ball. Wiz, running behind Terry and to his left, was announcing with a shout that he was open for a pass, and he was stating his position: trailing Terry, to Terry's left. In such a situation, Terry could drop off a pass to Wiz without even looking back. He could drop it off blind.

It was a natural. Time was running out for Terry. The defenders were moving in on him. And Wiz, as usual, was in good position, and he was there at the right moment. Terry, laying the ball off to his left, would send Wiz veering wide of the defenders, perhaps to find an opening for a shot on goal.

To his right, Terry saw Bones race into view. The little center forward was dancing in jerky motions around a defender and heading for open space at the edge of the penalty area. The Linden defenders in front of Terry split slightly. They were spreading out to cover Wiz to Terry's left and the approaching threat of Bones to Terry's right.

In that instant, Terry saw a flash of an opening through the Linden defenders. They were off-balance and moving the wrong way. Beyond the Linden fullbacks, he saw the figure of the Linden goalie, confused by the three-pronged attack—Terry, with the ball, and Wiz and Bones—coming

136

at him. The goalie was standing flat-footed in the goal mouth, jerking his head from side to side, trying to keep an eye on all three threats at the same time.

Terry weighed his chances. He figured that once through the slot between the defenders, he faced a clear shot on goal, with an uncertain goalie feeling himself tugged in all directions. One fake and a kick—and goal. The goalie would be duck soup.

Terry danced into the opening between the defenders with the ball. Suddenly the opening was not there. At the last moment, the fullbacks closed ranks on Terry. Seemingly, they had read his mind. Off-balance and heading the wrong way a moment ago, they were now in Terry's path and ready to tackle him. Terry collided with a wall of arms and legs. The ball squirted away, to Terry's left. Wiz, racing in, made a stab for it, but too late. A Linden defender had already swung a sturdy leg and sent the ball sailing high and far back into the safe territory at midfield.

Terry moaned and turned to race back upfield. "Nice try," he called out to Wiz.

Wiz smiled weakly, shrugged, and ran toward the action at midfield.

Moving into position, Terry's eyes met Bones's for an instant. They were flashing with anger. He shouted, "I was open."

Then they were separated in their rush toward the melee around the ball.

Yes, Bones had been open. So had Wiz been. But the

137

defense was closing in on both of them. There was a crack between the two Linden fullbacks. Terry had seen it. The crack seemed wide enough. So he was wrong. He made a mistake. So what? All players make mistakes. They miscalculate. Nobody is perfect. Wiz understood.

Terry glanced at Bones, now slowing in his pursuit as the Linden Tigers moved the ball across the halfway line. "Sour grapes," Terry said to himself. "Sure Bones wanted me to pass to him, so he could score. Sour grapes."

Chapter 15

Only minutes later Terry scored the first goal of the match.

He was moving out toward the halfway line, watching the wild scramble for the ball at the edge of the center circle. The ball came trickling out of the crowd of players. Terry started for it. Suddenly Miguel Toledano, the shorter of the Mexican boys, came out of nowhere and swung a foot into the ball. He hit it squarely. The ball took off on a line. Terry screeched to a halt. Then Wiz, leaping and turning, got himself in front of the ball. With perfect timing, he arched his back and snapped his head forward, sending the ball back toward Terry. Terry, with two quick steps to his left, took in the pass.

Terry was fifteen yards in from the touchline, just outside the penalty area.

Immediately two of the tough Linden defenders were on him. Out of the corner of his eye, Terry saw Bones running a weaving pattern in front of the goal, waving his arms frantically. There was no room for Terry to pass with the two defenders swarming over him.

Terry turned quickly, dribbling with his right foot, and eluded one of the defenders. The other defender stuck with Terry as he drove toward the goal, veering into a line parallel to the goal line. Bones was behind him now. He heard Bones shout something. The defender marking Terry was matching him step for step.

Driving through from the side, Terry stopped suddenly, his foot atop the ball. The Linden player marking him, surprised by Terry's abrupt halt, ran helplessly on past, leaving Terry in the open. The Linden goalie, too, was pulled out of position by Terry's sudden stop. The defender marking Terry turned frantically and tried to recover. The goalie screeched to a halt and scrambled back. But it was too late for both of them. Terry had whipped them, and he knew it. He had the instant of freedom that he needed. In the moment of the opening, he swung his right foot through, sending the ball rocketing toward the goal.

Terry, keeping his head down, knew the shot was good without looking. He could feel it.

The cheers roared down from the bleachers. Terry looked up in time to see the ball coming off the net and hitting the ground. He shot both fists into the air and let out a cheer.

Bones, nearby, made no move to run over for a slap on the back. He turned upfield to position himself for the goalie's kick resuming the play.

Terry frowned at Bones. Again Bones had wanted the pass and the shot on goal. But again Terry had taken the shot. The coach had said, "Shoot, shoot, shoot." So Terry had shot. And this time Terry had scored.

"Sour grapes," Terry told himself.

Archie McAlister, racing over from right forward, embraced Terry and swung him around. Wiz and Jorge, who had been running in from midfield to support the drive on goal, caught Terry at the same time with a huge hug, pounding him on the back and shouting.

Terry, grinning, hugged them back and knew this was the best moment for him of the nine matches of the Windsor Eagles.

Through the remainder of the first half, Wiz and his partners at midfield, Paul Chandler and Jorge, fought a valiant holding action against the two skillful Mexican boys. They booted the ball long and high toward Windsor's forward line at every opportunity, giving Terry and Bones and Archie the edge that Horst Schmidt's strategy called for.

But the Eagles were unable to convert the strategy into more goals. The two Mexican boys seemed to be everywhere. Terry tangled with one or the other of them time and again, as they raced back under one of the Windsor halfbacks' high kicks to bolster the defense. Every time they succeeded in thwarting the Eagles' attack on goal.

Terry felt a growing sense of frustration as the teams rocked back and forth on the field.

The Tigers successfully defused one of the most dangerous weapons in the Eagles' arsenal, the corner kick. Obviously well-versed in the Eagles' strong points, the Tigers brought up both Camacho and Toledano to the goal mouth for corner kicks. The accurate corner kicks of Wiz and the fearsome heading of Terry, so effective in past matches, went for naught. Wiz's kicks were accurate, as always. But the Mexican boys, particularly Camacho, the taller one, bottled Terry up every time. The Tigers had done their homework.

At the other end of the field, the Mexican boys pounded away at the Windsor goal from twenty yards out—hard, accurate shots. Each one was dangerous, at best a possible goal, at worst a setup for the Linden forwards. Henrik Sterner and the fullbacks, with Wiz dropping back to help, raced furiously, trying to mark the Linden attackers. They had their hands full fending off the barrage. But Hank Dodsworth always seemed to be in the right place for a save when a skittering shot eluded the back line or a forward got an open shot on goal.

At the half time the score stood: Eagles 1, Tigers 0.

The Eagles' dressing room was a quiet place. The players

142

sat slumped on benches, breathing heavily. They were out front on the scoreboard, but only barely. They had seen enough of the Linden Tigers to know that one goal was not going to mean victory. The Eagles needed more goals, and the goals were not coming easily.

Horst Schmidt let the players take their drinks of water, towel off the sweat, and rest. Then he stepped into the center of the dressing-room floor. First he outlined a possible change in strategy for the second half to meet what he expected from the Tigers.

"They are not going to let us get away with the long kicks to the forwards all night without changing something to stop us," he said. "I'm surprised they haven't done so before now. It just shows they have confidence in their system. But in the second half I suspect they will do something—probably shift people around—to stop us." He paused. "If this happens, we will lose our strong advantage at the forwards, and at the same time we will gain an advantage at midfield. If they do shift their strength—that is, Camacho and Toledano—that is the time to go back to a more conservative game. Work the ball in carefully. Draw them out. Understand?"

Some of the players nodded unconsciously. Others, like Terry, sat motionless, watching the coach.

Then Schmidt, as always at the half time, began citing the errors of the first half. Speaking softly and matter-of-factly, Schmidt was brutal, and the German accent some-

143

how made his words more cutting. He named names, sparing no one. He described the errors—and what should have been done instead—in painful detail.

Even after eight matches, Terry was not used to the coach's calmly delivered, blistering critiques. On the football team, the raging of Wilson Brundage when things were not going well always rolled off Terry easily, as it did the other football players. But Schmidt's cool dissection of a player's performance was something to be dreaded. Terry knew the others felt the same way.

Schmidt mentioned hurried kicks that went awry, losing the Eagles the possession of the ball. He pointed to instances of indecision causing delays that enabled the opponent to regroup. He listed failures to center—and keep centering—as directed.

The players, when cited, nodded their heads in understanding. They did not reply to the criticism. Horst Schmidt brooked no excuses, and everyone knew it.

Only Hank, with his series of great saves in the goal mouth and his booming kicks backing the Tigers to the halfway line, came in for undiluted praise from the coach. "Keep it up in the second half," Schmidt told him.

The goalie, leaning back with his arms folded over his chest, nodded and murmured, "Yeah," grinning. He acted not so much as one acknowledging a salute but as the good-humored yet skeptical recipient of instructions to walk to the moon.

144

"You can do it," Schmidt said, reading Hank's reaction.

Schmidt turned to Terry. "You tried to dribble through a crowd out there when you had two teammates open for a pass," he said. "In the early minutes. You remember. That was dumb. You know it was dumb. Use your head for something other than taking a shot at the ball."

Terry nodded. He was thinking of his goal, not the thwarted shot that had come earlier. But as he looked at the coach in silence, he knew that Horst Schmidt would find no time in this intermission to issue a compliment on Terry's goal. He knew what Horst Schmidt was thinking: the score might be 2–0 instead of 1–0, if Terry had passed off.

From the end of the bench where Terry was sitting, Bones Nelson broke the silence unexpectedly. "Showboating," he said.

The word, spoken softly, jerked Terry back from his thoughts of the goal to the memory of the bad play and Bones's angry eyes. Terry flushed and glared down the line at the slender little forward. Bones was sitting forward, elbows on knees, staring at the floor. He seemed to have been speaking more to himself than to the room full of players. But in the silence of the room the word came through as a shout.

Terry opened his mouth, but no words came out. He was flabbergasted. He remembered Hank's words: "It shows." Bones had been wanting to say "showboating" since

145

the season started. Now he had said it. How many others in the room wanted to say it?

Terry had the horrible feeling that everyone in the room —everyone in the world—was watching him. Terry kept his eyes on Bones. Bones kept his eyes on the floor.

In the moment of startled silence that followed Bones's remark, the whispering voice of Wiz, leaning toward Henrik, could be heard, "What is showboating?"

The question, heard clearly throughout the silent dressing room, brought a nervous smile to some faces. Others, grim-faced, stared at the floor without moving.

Henrik raised his eyebrows and rolled his eyes toward the ceiling. His expression clearly stated that he did not intend to try to answer Wiz's question.

Terry waited for someone—Schmidt or maybe Hank— to speak up. If they thought Bones was wrong, somebody would speak up and say so. But for a moment that seemed an hour, nobody spoke.

Then Schmidt snapped, "That's enough of that!" The coach was glaring at Bones. Then he turned his gaze over the entire dressing room. The nervous smiles vanished. The players stared at the floor or watched the coach with deadpan expressions. They sat motionless. Wiz alone moved. He seemed puzzled by the outburst. He twisted in his seat on the bench and looked around the room.

Terry found his voice. "Coach said to shoot, and that's what I was doing—shooting," he said. He hoped he sounded angry. He knew he didn't. The words sounded to him like a whine, a plea. He was sorry he had spoken.

Another moment seemed like an hour. Nobody spoke. Then Schmidt turned to Terry. "Cut it!" he said. "Cut it right now!"

Terry glowered at the coach but kept his mouth shut.

After another moment of strained silence, Schmidt resumed his critique of the first half. Terry heard none of it. He stared blankly at a spot on the wall behind the coach. Nobody had come to his defense. Nobody had shot Bones down. Were they going to let Bones get away with it? Did they agree with him? Terry felt very alone in the room full of players.

Finally Schmidt said, "Time to go."

Chapter 16

Terry stood up. Looking at no one, he marched toward the door and crowded through with the other players. The corridor seemed a blur. Then they pushed their way through the outside door and stepped into the darkness at the end of the playing field. The players were all in shadows. Terry, staring straight ahead, saw none of them. Ahead of them, the crowd in the bleachers was a splash of wild color under the arc lights.

Horst Schmidt jogged around the group of players and headed for the playing field. "Let's go," he said.

Terry and the others broke into a trot behind him.

Crossing the goal line, the thought hit Terry, I scored the only goal of the match. Okay, so I lost the ball on a shot that did not work. Bones wanted the pass so he could score the goal himself. Next time, too, when I scored, Bones wanted a pass so he could get the goal for himself. Now he calls it showboating. Sour grapes! And the others let it stand. Nobody called Bones down for saying it. Sour grapes! It's the showboater—me—who has the Eagles out front on the scoreboard. Me, just me. If they don't like it, that's just tough. I'll show them what showboating is.

Terry and the others reached the bench.

Hank, jogging up alongside Terry, said, "Don't let Bones bother you."

"Don't worry."

"He's just got this funny—"

Terry stuck his face up close to Hank's face. He wanted to ask, "Where were you when all of that was going on in the dressing room?" But instead he repeated, "Don't worry about it."

He picked a ball from the cluster at the bench and dribbled onto the field, joining the brief warm-up before the start of the second half.

Off to the side, he saw Horst Schmidt and Bones standing together, away from the others. Schmidt was doing the talking. Bones was nodding his head, a serious expression on his face.

"Who cares?" Terry said to himself, and booted a practice shot at the goal.

Before the second half was thirty seconds old, the accuracy of Horst Schmidt's prediction about Linden's strategy was clearly evident on the field. The Tigers were making radical changes in their game plan. Camacho moved from halfback to fullback. His assignment, obviously, was to break up the play of Terry and Bones and Archie receiving the long kicks from midfield. Terry frowned, knowing the second half was sure to be tougher than the first half.

The change in the Linden lineup left Wiz moving with a newfound freedom at midfield. No longer was Wiz harassed at every turn by a pair of expert duelers. No longer did he find himself double-teamed on offense and defense. Toledano, remaining in midfield, was tough enough, to be sure. But Wiz was his match, and the master of the other two Linden halfbacks. The Eagles shifted their game back to a ball-control strategy.

Terry had every reason to wish Wiz well at midfield. The more damage Wiz could wreak at midfield, the quicker the Tigers would be forced to move Camacho back to halfback and out of Terry's way.

With Horst Schmidt gesturing them into place from the sideline, Terry and Bones and Archie moved several paces toward midfield. Their presence backed up the halfbacks, adding support to Wiz and Jorge and Paul. The Tigers' midfield, already weakened by the transfer of Camacho to fullback, was outnumbered a bit more by the looming presence of the Eagles' forwards. Horst Schmidt wanted to drive Camacho out of the fullback slot and back to halfback.

Camacho clung to Terry like wallpaper. At every turn, the Mexican boy was there, marking Terry tightly. With every maneuver, Camacho followed Terry as if the two of them were performing a well-rehearsed dance step. The few times that Terry came up with the ball he barely managed to get away a wobbly pass to Bones, who was quickly covered by the Linden defenders, or back to Wiz at midfield.

Gradually the match settled into a frantic battle at midfield.

Twice, at the other end of the field, the Tigers broke through, stabbing deep into Windsor territory, threatening to score. Each time Henrik, with help from Chuck Horton, bottled up the Tigers and took the ball away.

Then, with the second half more than ten minutes old, Wiz sent a long shot booming toward the nets from thirty yards out. A Linden defender, going high, partially blocked the shot. The ball went bounding high into the air—straight up—in front of the goal mouth.

Players converged from all sides. For the Tigers, there was extreme danger. For the Eagles, there was magnificent opportunity. Nothing short of a goal itself was better for the offense than a wildly bounding ball in the mouth of the

151

opponents' goal. Anyone might kick it in, even a desperately lunging defender. It was a goalie's nightmare. From a crowd of players so close in, only blind luck would enable the goalie to be in position to stop a shot on goal.

Terry raced in, eyeing the ball, now starting to come down. Somebody bumped him. He regained his stride, watching the ball in its descent. Camacho was at Terry's elbow. Terry left the ground. He was between Camacho and the falling ball. He bowed his body and snapped his head forward. He felt the impact of the ball on his forehead. The ball went whistling into the corner of the nets.

Coming down, Terry tumbled to his knees. And there, before getting up, he shot his fists into the air and shouted, "Goal!"

Archie McAlister fell on Terry with a hug. Wiz, whose long shot had set up the goal, lifted Terry to his feet and shouted, "Goal! Goal!"

Terry heard the cheers rolling down the bleachers from both sides of the field and the shouting and whooping of his teammates. He did not see Bones Nelson and he did not look for him.

"Like it or not, there it is—two goals, the only two goals in the match," he told himself. "Bones, what do you—and all the rest of you too—what do you think of that?"

He looked at Archie and Wiz, still hanging on him, pounding him on the back. Downfield, he saw Henrik skipping in an elated victory dance. Paul Chandler was shouting something. Terry was smiling. The goal felt good. But even better was the feeling, "I showed 'em."

Terry's goal seemed to set the course of the match. The Tigers were less tight in their marking, less alert on defense. They had less punch on the attack.

Minutes later Bones, playing off a pass from Terry twelve yards out, drilled the ball into the nets, lifting the Eagles to an astonishing 3–0 lead over the powerhouse Linden Tigers.

From there, the Eagles worked the clock, dribbling and passing, playing the ball-control game, letting the minutes tick away the Tigers' diminishing chances.

Only in the waning minutes of the match did the Tigers finally get on the scoreboard. Toledano, the shorter and quicker of the two Mexican boys, still playing at halfback, stole the ball from Paul Chandler near the touchline thirty yards out. Dribbling brilliantly, he raced between Woody Clark and Chuck Horton, heading for Henrik Sterner. Henrik, weary after the long night of chasing and pounding, let Toledano escape him. Toledano came out the other side with the ball and, with a perfect shoulder fake, forced Hank to commit himself to his left in the mouth of the goal. Then he booted the ball to the other side. The bullet kick sailed past Hank's frantic lunge.

But by that time the issue was settled, and the final score was 3–1.

* * *

"You can showboat any time you want!"

Only Henrik Sterner could say it and get away with it. Standing with a towel wrapped around his waist, leaning forward in an exaggerated pose, he shouted the wisecrack at Terry.

Everybody in the room laughed.

Terry grinned back at Henrik.

"Showboat," Wiz piped gleefully.

Terry smiled at him.

"Fannn-tastic!" Hank shouted. "You were fantastic."

Terry grinned at Hank.

The grin on Terry's face was real. The cheers, the shouts, the laughter—all for him—did feel good. The game had been exhilarating—two goals and one assist in the biggest victory of the season. It all felt good. But behind the grin, Terry could not shake the sickening memory of that one word, *showboating*, uttered by Bones at the half time. Worse yet, he remembered the silence that followed. Nobody had come to his defense. All had kept their mouths shut. Somebody should have let Bones have it. Nobody did.

Now, as he looked around the happy dressing room, they were cheering him. But not one of them—Henrik, Wiz, even Hank—had spoken up for him. They had let Bones say it, unchallenged. They had let him get away with it. All of them, every last one of them. Maybe they all agreed with Bones. Terry had been sure, until that terrible moment when Bones spoke, that he was succeeding

154

in yielding the spotlight to Wiz with good grace. But maybe not. Hank had said, "It shows." Maybe it did. And maybe they were all glad to have Bones put the star—of football, of basketball, of baseball—in his place.

Terry felt his smile fading. He wanted to shout, "You ain't seen nothin' yet. If you think that was showboating, just watch." He clamped the smile back in place.

Where was Bones? Was he, of all people, joining in the cheering and shouting and laughing over Terry's performance?

As if the thought were a signal, Bones materialized suddenly at Terry's side. "I want to apologize," he said softly.

Terry turned to him. He kept the smile on his face. "Forget it," he said.

"I shouldn't have said it," Bones said.

"Don't worry about it," Terry said. He was still smiling. Terry stepped around Bones and walked into the shower.

Hank followed Terry into the shower. "Was Bones apologizing?"

"Yeah."

Bob Traynor and Jorge Perez walked into the shower, ending the conversation.

As Terry lathered his body with the soap and then rinsed off, he remembered the scene at the sideline: Horst Schmidt lecturing Bones, Bones nodding. "Sure, Bones apologized," Terry said to himself.

Back at his locker, toweling off, Terry was no longer

smiling. Some of the players already had dressed and left. Others were still in the shower. Terry could hear Henrik's voice from the shower.

Horst Schmidt walked over to Terry. "You played an outstanding game," he said.

Terry looked up. "Thanks," he said.

Schmidt dropped onto the bench next to Terry. He turned and leaned back, lifting a foot to the bench. "I saw Bones talking with you," he said. "Did he apologize?"

Terry wanted to say, "Yes, just the way you told him to." But all he said was, "Yes."

"I am sure that he was sincere," Schmidt said. "Those things get said—whether they are meant or not—in the heat of an important match."

"Sure."

Schmidt got to his feet. "Try to forget it," he said.

"Sure."

Chapter 17

The next ten days, and the three matches spread among them, were a time of victorious elation for the Windsor Eagles.

The three opponents, none as tough as the Linden Tigers, fell—the Ridgeway Pirates by a 3–1 score, the Elmwood Plainsmen by 4–0, the Crampton Cardinals by 5–2.

With twelve straight victories under their belts, the Windsor Eagles were riding high. The crowds, which had been growing steadily, were now filling the bleachers at away matches as well as at home. The Windsor fans who had driven to the neighboring suburbs for the Eagles' road games frequently outnumbered the home-team fans. The Windsor cheerleaders continued to turn out in full force. At school, Terry and Bones and Wiz and Hank and all the others were the heroes of the classrooms and the corridors. Suddenly soccer was important at Windsor High.

Even Horst Schmidt seemed pleased. True, the coach's worries about the dangers of the upcoming match always overshadowed the delights of the last victory. But he was showing a glint in his eye. Horst Schmidt was a winner again.

But for Terry the spectacular success of the team, the cheers of the crowds, the enthusiasm of the student body were beginning to ring hollow as the days passed. He had earned the thrill of victory. He had earned the cheers of the crowd. He had earned the headlines in the *Windsor Bulletin* and the shouted greetings of "Great game, Terry" in the corridors. He had earned the goals, too, because he was shooting, shooting, shooting.

But he also had earned the watchful eye and the warning words of Horst Schmidt. And, more and more as the matches rolled by, he had earned the frowns of his teammates.

Terry had started the match with the Ridgeway Pirates determined to hold the starring role he had captured in the Linden match two nights earlier. If Bones wanted to call it showboating, so be it. If the others on the team felt

158

the same as Bones, so be it. If Horst Schmidt called it taking dumb shots, so be it. Terry had given up pretending he didn't care about stardom. His plan was to shoot, shoot, shoot.

Through the first half Terry pounded away at the goal every time he got the ball. He backed off his plan only when he heard the clipped German accent from the sideline, "Pass it off! Pass it off!" Then a few moments later he was back at it: shoot, shoot, shoot. He got one goal in the first half, and the Eagles led 1–0.

Terry took his lumps in the dressing room. "You are taking too many dumb shots," Schmidt told him. "Look around for a teammate. Pass it off when you're bottled up."

Terry waited for Bones—or someone—to say it: showboating. So what? But Terry himself was the one who broke the silence. "Can't win without scoring; can't score without shooting."

The dressing room was quiet.

Terry grinned, thinking to himself, I scored the only goal we've got.

Schmidt stared at Terry for a moment. Then, as if Terry had not spoken at all, Schmidt resumed his critique of the first half's play.

In the opening minutes of the second half, Terry challenged a Ridgeway halfback at the touchline just short of midfield. He won the duel and came away with the ball, bringing the crowd to its feet with a roar. Terry felt a thrill as he dribbled away from the befuddled Ridgeway player toward the center of the field. He eluded one Ridgeway defender and faked another out of his path. Advancing toward the penalty arc, he spotted Bones waving frantically for a pass. But Terry drove another couple of yards toward the goal. He eyed the Ridgeway goalie. The goalie was sure to move over to cover Bones. The goalie was certain to think that Bones, in the open, would be receiving a pass.

Instead, Terry planted his left foot and booted the ball toward the nets. His foot told him the kick on goal was perfect—a solid hit. But when he looked up from the kick he saw the ball might be going a shade too high. And worse, he saw that the goalie had held his ground. The goalie had not committed himself to his left to guard against the danger of Bones taking a pass. The goalie leaped and got his fingertips on the ball. The rising ball glanced off his fingertips, bounced off the cross-bar, and sailed out-of-bounds past the goal line.

Terry heard the disappointed moan of the crowd.

The raspy voice of Owen Milliman announced on the loudspeaker, "A shot by Terry Masters . . . misses!"

Terry glanced at Schmidt on the sideline. The coach's expression showed nothing. But he was patting Butch Sterling on the rump and sending him onto the field to replace Terry.

Terry trotted off the field. He was due a rest anyway.

A few minutes later, panting on the sideline while Butch played in his place, Terry found Schmidt standing at his elbow.

"How many times do I have to tell you?" Schmidt said. He was not angry. Terry had never seen Schmidt angry. But the words, though softly spoken, seemed to have a cutting edge to them. "That was a dumb shot," he said. "You are taking too many of them."

"I thought the goalie was moving over to cover Bones," Terry said, keeping his eyes on the action on the field.

"But he didn't," Schmidt said. "Bones was open. Bones could have scored."

Terry shrugged. "Okay," he said. "I made a mistake." Schmidt held Terry on the sideline for ten minutes before sending him back into the match, where he scored his second goal—the Eagles' third goal—clinching the victory.

Again the cheers in the dressing room belonged to Terry. There was no denying him the credit. He had scored two of the Eagles' three goals. But Schmidt passed Terry up as he circled the room congratulating his winners.

Over the weekend, around the town, more cheers came to Terry. His name was in the headline of the *Windsor Bulletin*. The picture alongside the story showed Terry socking home his first goal. Wiz's name was not in the headline. Terry's was. Wiz's picture was not there. Terry's was. Wiz was playing as well as ever—and Terry knew it—and Bones also was playing as well as ever. But in the

161

face of Terry's new strategy, neither of them could edge into the spotlight occupied by Terry.

At the drugstore, at Herbie's Place, at the record shop, everywhere, people called out to Terry, "Great game!" Terry smiled and waved back at them, friends and strangers alike. The spotlight, gone for so long, felt good. Hank had said Terry missed the spotlight. Hank had been correct. Let Wiz—and Bones too—have a taste of how it felt to see the applause go to someone else, no matter how well they played. Hank had said, "It shows." Well, Terry was not worrying about that anymore. So Bones called it showboating. So maybe the others agreed with him. So what? They still had to cheer. Terry decided to keep the spotlight.

The only discordant note of the weekend came late on Saturday night. Terry and Hank were seated across from each other in a booth at Herbie's Place. They had been to a movie—the latest in the John Wayne Film Festival at the Windsor Theater—and had stopped off for Cokes before going home.

"Schmidt jerked you out of the game the other night," Hank said.

Terry glanced at Hank. He thought, Not another lecture, please. But he said, "I needed a few minutes' rest."

"What did he say?"

Terry raised his eyebrows. Was it so obvious, even from Hank's distant station in the goal mouth, that the coach was criticizing Terry? Terry had not thought so.

162

"That old stuff about a dumb shot," he said.

Hank did not speak for a moment. Then he said, "He kept you on the sideline for ten minutes."

"Yeah." Terry paused. "I don't know, maybe he wanted to give Butch some playing time."

On Tuesday, when the players boarded the bus at the school for the short drive to Elmwood and their match with the Plainsmen, a caravan of cars more than two blocks long was lined up behind them. First behind the players' bus was the band bus. Behind the band was a station wagon carrying the cheerleaders. And then, stretching all the way back to where the road bent around the football field, were cars with fans ready to see their Eagles win their eleventh straight match.

To Terry, it seemed like the good old days of football.

The Plainsmen, with their record of seven victories and three defeats, owed their success to a canny and innovative coach. They had no players of the caliber of Wiz or Terry or even Bones. Man for man, the Eagles had them outgunned.

"But I warn you," Schmidt told the players in the dressing room before boarding the bus, "you will see tactics and deceptions you've never seen before. They may lack an outstanding player, but they can beat you with their brains."

For Terry, the warning was not long in coming true. The first time he got the ball—a pass from Bones—he whirled and took aim on the goal. He never got the shot off. Suddenly, from nowhere, four Plainsmen swarmed him. Terry held onto the ball, tried to break through the crowd of stabbing feet, and in the end lost the ball to one of them.

Three more times it happened.

Time and again Terry saw Bones with the ball—once poking in a goal—and he saw Archie with the ball, marked by only one or two Plainsmen. But the Plainsmen were pulling in two halfbacks from midfield to join two fullbacks in marking Terry.

Terry had been a marked man on the athletic field before, so it was not a strange experience. In football, opposing linemen keyed on him. In basketball, he had been double-teamed. But the Plainsmen were more than keying on him. They were more than double-teaming him. They were pulling defense strength off Bones and weakening themselves at midfield to bottle up Terry. It did not make sense.

At the half time, thanks to Bones's short shot for a goal and a brilliant dribble and shot on the dead run by Wiz, the Eagles led 2–0.

For Terry, there were no goals. For Terry, there were no shots on goal. He never, in the midst of the crowd of thrashing opponents, even managed to get off a shot. Worse yet, he lost the ball to the Plainsmen on each of the four occasions they swarmed him.

"What's going on out there?" he blurted in the dressing room.

164

"It's quite clear," Schmidt said. "They scouted our last match or two. They know that you won't pass off. They know that you always shoot on goal. So they're swarming you, and while you are still trying to take a shot on goal, they are taking the ball away from you."

Terry gritted his teeth.

"Can't score without shooting," Bones said softly, smiling as he quoted Terry.

"Whose side are you on?" Terry barked.

"Whose side are *you* on?"

"Cut it out," Schmidt said. He paused. The room was silent. "Fortunately, their tactic has not hurt us seriously."

Terry glared at the coach. Terry Masters was not used to hearing that his being rendered ineffective was anything but a very serious loss.

In the second half, Terry tried once more to break through the wall of Elmwood defenders, to score, to show them that their tactic was not working. Beating them at their own game would make them go away. It was the only way.

But he lost the ball again, and Schmidt sent Butch in to replace him.

"A dumb play," Schmidt said. "When will you learn?"

Terry hardly glanced at the coach. He was scoreless, true, but the threat of his repeated pounding at the goal was freeing his teammates. Terry preferred making the goals himself. No doubt about it, the Elmwood strategy was frustrating. But the coach ought to know the value of a serious danger in one quarter freeing players elsewhere on the field. Surely the coach did know. But all he kept saying was, "Dumb play." Terry frowned.

The match was nearly over and the Eagles far out front with a 4–0 score, when Terry went back onto the field. Nobody passed to him, and he did not handle the ball.

Even so the headline the next morning was Terry's: *Masters Boxed in but Eagles Prevail 4–0.*

Neither the newspaper nor Terry took note of the fact that nobody passed to him in the closing minutes of the match.

The Crampton match was ten minutes old, and still scoreless, before Terry got possession of the ball. Elbow to elbow with Bones in a wild scramble with the Cardinals for the ball, Terry came out with it in front of the goal. In the frantic flailing, Terry had the ball for an instant before anyone around him realized it. In that instant, with his quickness, Terry slammed the ball into the nets for a goal.

"Nice," Bones said.

Terry, surprised, grinned at him. The play had been a good one, he knew. A moment's hesitation and he would have been swamped by defenders. An instant's delay would have found the goalie standing in front of him. Yes, a good play. Even Bones had to admit it.

Afterward, Terry shot and missed four times. Twice

166

the goalie speared long shots. One kick barely left his foot before a defender deflected it. The fourth, a bad kick, sailed over the goal.

Bones was silent now. He frowned at Terry when he looked at him at all.

Wiz, too, was wearing a frown of disapproval.

By half time the Eagles were leading 3–1, thanks to a short kick by Archie from the side and a driving charge down the middle by Wiz. But to Terry there seemed to be more frowns than smiles among the Eagles.

Early in the second half Terry got a shot, from twelve yards out, with a Cardinal marking him closely. The kick, hurried, went wide and the Cardinals recovered the ball.

Minutes later Wiz, dribbling in from midfield, split Bones and Terry before the Plainsmen converged on him and stopped him just outside the goal area. Wiz never even looked at Terry. He passed off to Bones at the edge of the goal. Bones booted it home for a goal.

"I was open," Terry called out to Wiz, now circling back to midfield to receive the goalie's kick resuming the play.

"So was Bones," Wiz answered over his shoulder.

Terry blinked.

Twice more Wiz passed off to Bones with hardly a glance at Terry, and once Archie McAlister, trapped, sent an awkward pass to Bones when a pass to Terry would have been easier.

"You're freezing me out," Terry complained to Wiz.

"Freezing?"

"You're not passing to me."

"You always kick the ball away," Wiz said. He spoke the words softly and simply, with a shrug, as if stating a fact obvious to all.

Terry, lying back, watching the action at the other end of the field, glanced at the sideline. Horst Schmidt, instead of watching the play near the Eagles' goal, was eyeing the forward area—Terry—and saying something to Butch.

Butch replaced Terry.

Walking home, Terry turned to Hank. "You saw it, didn't you? They were freezing me out."

Hank took a deep breath. "Not exactly," he said.

"What do you mean, not exactly. A freeze-out is a freeze-out."

"You're not going to like this."

"What?"

Hank stopped under a streetlight where they were parting to head their separate ways. Terry stood with him, hands thrust into the hip pockets of his jeans.

"Look at it this way: they're not freezing you out. It's been exactly the opposite. You've been freezing them out."

"What?"

"Well, you never pass to them. You always shoot. Isn't that a freeze-out, when you don't pass to them?"

* * *

By Monday morning, when he left home in the clear, crisp autumn weather for the nine-block walk to school, Terry had made up his mind.

In the darkness of his room before he fell asleep on Saturday night, in church on Sunday morning, at the auto show with his father in the afternoon, Terry kept hearing remarks: Hank's "It shows," and, "You're freezing *them* out," Horst Schmidt's "Dumb shot. When are you going to learn?" His father's "Pressure, pressure applied by yourself." And yes, there was Bones Nelson's "Showboater." Alone in his bed, he put all the remarks together.

Yes, he had expected to be the star of the soccer team, same as he had been star of the football team. Yes, he had been disappointed when Krystian Wisniewski showed up to capture the spotlight. And yes, he had to admit finally, it showed—to Hank, to his father, to everyone. It showed, too, to Horst Schmidt. Terry could see that now.

It must have shown most of all when Bones had blurted out "Showboater." Terry, instructed to shoot, shoot, shoot, had gone for the goal. Schmidt, always the sharp critic, had called it a dumb shot. It was a dumb shot. Terry knew. But then Bones, certain for a month that Terry Masters— Big Star Masters—couldn't stand the shadows, called it showboating.

Terry heard Fred shuffling around in the terrarium. Then his thoughts returned to worry at the remarks that were haunting him. He gritted his teeth. He had not been showboating. At least, he didn't think so. But Bones had

169

been sure for a month, so he said it. Maybe Bones was right.

No, Bones was wrong at that moment in the Linden match. But since then, stupidly, he had proven Bones right.

The pressure, the self-applied pressure his father had talked about, left him believing that everyone, Schmidt included, agreed with Bones. So he played the game without them—without his teammates, without Schmidt—and he proved Bones right.

"Stupid," Terry said aloud to no one but Fred in the darkness, and finally dropped off to sleep.

The worry was gone from Terry's mind and he was whistling, when he arrived at the school building and pulled open the front door to step into the lobby.

He could hardly wait for the day's classes to pass, for practice that afternoon, and then the Tuesday night match with the Hillcrest Broncos.

Chapter 18

"Terry, I have decided to start Butch Sterling in place of you at the left forward position against the Hillcrest Broncos tomorrow night."

Horst Schmidt, seated on a bench in the dressing room, now empty of all but the coach and Terry, spoke the words as casually as if he were commenting on the weather. The statement, spoken so matter-of-factly, took a moment to sink in on Terry, seated on a bench across from the coach.

When Horst Schmidt had approached Terry, dressing at his locker, the sweat of the practice session washed away

171

in the shower, and asked him to remain a moment behind the others, Terry had not been surprised. Neither had he been concerned. He was relieved, for he wanted to talk to the coach. He was anxious to proclaim the good news of the solution to the problem.

The coach's words hit Terry like a splash of cold water in the face.

"Since you have been the starter in our first twelve matches, I felt that you had a right to know of my decision before I announce the starting lineup at match time tomorrow night," Schmidt said.

Terry could not speak. His mouth worked but no words came out.

"This is best for the team," Schmidt said.

"But. . . ."

Schmidt smiled. It was a small, gentle smile. Terry had seen it before, and he grimaced. Coaches all seemed to use the same small, gentle smile when delivering bad news. It was meant to reassure.

"You will get some playing time against the Broncos tomorrow night," Schmidt said. "But you will not start the match, not be in the starting lineup."

The thoughts raced through Terry's mind. Terry Masters was being benched. What would his father think? What would the football players say? How would he meet Hank's eyes? And Bones? Bones was going to love this. Probably Wiz too.

Terry could think of nothing to say. He stared at the

coach in silence. Clearly Horst Schmidt had nothing more to say. He had made his announcement and assumed, apparently, that Terry knew full well the reasons for the change. That being so, there was no point in discussing reasons. No explanations, no regrets, no apologies. Horst Schmidt did not coddle his players—not on the practice field, not in a match, not even in the process of delivering a devastating statement. Terry waited, but he knew the coach had nothing more to say.

Schmidt got to his feet.

Terry stood too.

In the moment that they faced each other, standing in the aisle between the benches, Terry started to speak. He wanted to tell Schmidt that everything was changed now. He was no longer out for himself alone. He was a member of the team. Had Schmidt not noticed the new Terry Masters at the practice session just ended? Maybe. . . .

Terry took a deep breath. He forced a slight smile. "That sort of stuff—showboating—that's all over for me now. I figured it out for myself over the weekend. I've got my head screwed on right now." He paused. "There won't be any more of it—showboating. I promise."

The words sounded lame to Terry.

Schmidt sighed, as if in regret that Terry had made such a blatant plea for forgiveness. "Sit down," he said.

Terry and the coach faced each other from the benches again.

"First, Terry, let me say that the change in the starting

173

lineup will stand, as I have told you. I will not reverse my decision." Schmidt paused, keeping his eyes on Terry.

Terry felt a flush of embarrassment. He should have known there would be no talking Horst Schmidt out of the decision. He locked his hands together in his lap and squeezed hard. He had the feeling that he did not want to hear what Schmidt was about to say. He should have left the dressing room, saying no more, when they were standing. He wished he had left.

"Your attitude these last few matches has not only been detrimental to your own play, but—and I must always keep this in mind—has been detrimental to the team."

Terry sat, unmoving, his mouth a straight line, watching the coach.

"I have seen what is happening on the field, Terry. I am not blind, you know. And I have played this game of soccer myself, you know, so I can understand why players do some of the things they do.

"You have been taking dumb shots on goal. More of them with each passing match the last couple of weeks. I've told you so, but you would not listen. It seemed that you wanted all the goals for yourself.

"All that your dumb shots did was give the ball away. The more dumb shots you took, the less your teammates wanted to pass off the ball to you. It was as if, well, a pass to Terry Masters was the same as a pass being intercepted: no goal and the opponent got possession of the ball. So, more and more, your teammates were reluctant to pass the ball to you."

"I thought they were freezing me out," Terry said weakly.

"No, your teammates had lost confidence in you. It was understandable, I think. No, they were not freezing you out in the usual sense of the term. They were—consciously or unconsciously—doing the smart thing for the team. They had no confidence in you." Schmidt paused, seeming to want some comment from Terry.

"Yes," Terry said softly.

"And when that happens, Terry, do you know what becomes of your value to the team?"

Terry swallowed hard. He knew the answer. But he murmured, "What?"

"When that happens, Terry, you become useless to the Windsor Eagles. Your value to the team becomes zero. We find ourselves with one less player on the field for our team. We find ourselves, in effect, with only two forwards, not three, only ten players, not eleven, because one of our strikers cannot be given the ball."

"But I—"

Schmidt waved Terry into silence with a small move of his hand. "I know," he said. "I know that you have told me that you have changed your ways."

Terry nodded.

"It is not as simple as all that."

Terry waited.

"Terry, perhaps you can change your attitude"—Schmidt snapped his fingers—"just like that. But neither you nor I can change the attitude of your teammates that quickly. I can flick a switch on the wall there, and the lights will go off and on instantly. But people's feelings cannot be controlled so simply. Your teammates have an impression of you now, an impression that you created yourself, that was formed over a period of days, even weeks. That impression will not be changed by any statement from you, a promise, or even a speech. No words will change the impression. Only actions will change the impression."

Terry caught himself nodding his head slightly in agreement as Horst Schmidt spoke. Schmidt was correct, of course. Terry could hardly picture Bones Nelson listening to a promise and then saying, "Ah, sure, forget it, Terry ol' boy. Everything's fine now that you've said you've changed." Bones had believed the worst from the beginning. He was not going to believe a promise now. No way. And Wiz was not going to trade in his cold stare for a warm smile just for a spoken promise. Neither would Archie McAlister or any of the others. Probably even Hank, while wanting to accept Terry's word, would withhold final judgment until he saw what happened.

"You see, Terry, no matter how much you change your attitude, you are going to remain useless to your team until you—somehow—manage to change their attitude toward you. Or, to put it another way, until you succeed in restoring their confidence in you. That is what is lacking—confidence. You are going to have to win your way back onto the team, win your way back into the confidence of your teammates. You have to convince them by actions, not words, that you are playing for the team now, not for your own personal glory. There is nothing you can say and nothing that I, as the coach, can say that will accomplish this change in the minds of your teammates. Only action—your action—will make a difference."

Schmidt paused. He continued to watch Terry closely. "And, Terry," he said finally, "as long as you are useless to the team, you will not be the starting left forward."

"Yes," Terry said softly. He could think of nothing else to say.

Schmidt got to his feet again. "Now," he said, with the small smile back in place, "you had better be heading for home. And so must I. It is late."

Terry stood. "You said—"

"Yes, what?"

"You did say that I would get to play, though, didn't you?"

"You will get some playing time, yes."

Chapter 19

The stadium was packed to overflowing despite the afternoon's showers and the lingering threat of dark clouds. The fans were out in large numbers to see their Windsor High Eagles, undefeated and untied, go after their thirteenth straight triumph. The cheerleaders on the cinder track in front of the bleachers were stepping and clapping their hands in time to the blaring tune from the Windsor High band. From the press box atop the west bleachers, the raspy voice of Owen Milliman came over the public-address system, reading the scores of the Eagles' victories above the din of the crowd.

Owen Milliman was becoming more of a cheerleader for the Eagles with each passing match. Each score brought a small burst of applause from the fans who could hear him above their own chatter and the noise of the band. Overhead, the huge arc lights bathed the whole scene in a shadowless brightness.

At the north end of the field the Hillcrest Broncos, in their black-and-orange uniforms, were weaving through their warm-up drills. The Broncos, with a soccer program no older than the Eagles' program, did not present a formidable threat.

At the sideline at the south end of the field, Horst Schmidt was frowning at the sight of his Windsor Eagles dribbling, passing, and running through their warm-up.

For any fan glancing at the coach, the frown was nothing surprising. Horst Schmidt always frowned before—and during—a match, and sometimes even after the match had been logged in the victory column.

But on this night Horst Schmidt had reason to deepen the frown. He and the players had been met with stunning news when they arrived at the dressing room for the match. Henrik Sterner was at that moment in the emergency room at Windsor Memorial Hospital, waiting for a plaster cast to harden around his broken ankle. Henrik had bounced his moped over a curb one time too many. Halfway home from school at the end of classes, Henrik had cut too sharply coming off a curb. He fell. The skidding moped twisted and snapped his right ankle.

Perhaps the Hillcrest Broncos already had noticed that the sturdy figure wearing number fifty-eight, the pillar of the Eagles' defense, was missing from the field. In any case, they would know soon enough. The Eagles would be playing with a second stringer in the back line of their defense.

Henrik's absence was a dangerous chink in the armor for the Eagles. The sweeper, from his station in front of the goalie, commanded the best view of the field and roamed the largest section. He was the anchor of the defense and, at the same time, the starting point for an attack when the defense intercepted a pass. The job required the talents of a Henrik Sterner—mobility, speed, power, and kicking skill.

Horst Schmidt had not said so in the dressing room, but the sweeper was sure to be Henrik's normal substitute, Jimmy Robinson. Slow afoot, a bit on the awkward side, not blessed with the strengths and abilities of the natural athlete, Jimmy was all the Eagles had. For the Broncos, Henrik's absence at the sweeper position would be heartening news, an unexpected lift in their hopes of knocking off the undefeated Eagles.

All of it was reason enough to put a frown on Horst Schmidt's face.

Perhaps there was another reason, known only to Terry and the coach, that deepened the frown on Horst Schmidt's forehead. By decree of the coach, the Eagles would start the match with a second stringer at left forward. Butch Sterling would be there in place of Terry Masters. There would be a reduction in the firepower of the Eagles' attack.

When Terry first heard in the dressing room about Henrik's accident, he had wondered if the tragedy might save him from being benched. Perhaps Schmidt, faced with having one starter unavoidably out of the match, might decide against choosing to sideline another starter. The coach could change his mind. He could take Terry at his word that the showboating was over and gamble that the other players would be quick to see the change. While changing clothes for the match, Terry watched the coach. Horst Schmidt was moving around the dressing room, speaking a word to a player here and asking a question there. His face gave Terry his answer. Terry knew that the thought of reversing himself, no matter what, had never entered Horst Schmidt's mind. Butch Sterling would start at left forward, as stated to Terry the evening before. All that remained was the announcement.

Terry, taking his turn in the warm-ups at racing up for a pass and a shot on goal, grimaced at the thought of the moment when Schmidt would read the starting lineup.

Terry knew the reactions to expect from the other players. Butch Sterling, of course, would be excited. He would light up like an incandescent bulb. The others instinctively would turn their eyes to Terry. They would all look at him. The glances would not be sympathetic. Not

181

after the last couple of weeks. First, of course, they would be curious. How's he taking it? And then, because of some quirk in the human makeup, they would be relieved. They would all, even those who liked Terry and had not been involved in the hassle on the forward line, feel a sense of relief in his demotion. They would be relieved Terry was taking the humiliation of being benched and would be grateful they were not in his place. Terry had seen it happen before when a starter was sidelined. Probably Bones, and perhaps even Wiz, would be pleased. If so, it would show in their faces. Terry dreaded the moment of Horst Schmidt's announcement.

He had dreaded the moment, too, the night before when he broke the news to his father at the dinner table.

"Why?" his father asked, putting down his fork.

The question was a tough one for Terry to answer. He considered saying simply that Butch Sterling had beat him out for the starting position. In a way, that would be the truth. But Alvin Masters would never believe him. He had seen his son a star in every sport he played, and he would know that more was involved.

"Coach Schmidt says that I have been taking too many wild shots on goal," Terry said. Well, he thought, that was the reason, sort of. He shrugged slightly. "That's what he said," he added finally.

"And?" his father asked.

Another tough question to answer. Terry squirmed. He

182

glanced at his mother. She was interested, concerned, but no help. He wished now that he had not told his father. He wished he had put off this discussion. His father could have waited and found out when the starting lineup was announced at the match. That would not have been the fairest treatment of him, but Terry would have gained twenty-four hours before he had to explain.

"And?" Terry repeated his father's question.

"And what else? Taking too many wild shots on goal is no problem. One conversation—one word from the coach —and you can cut that out, can't you? I don't see the problem. I don't know that much about soccer, I'll admit, but taking too many wild shots on goal doesn't sound to me like a problem that is difficult to solve. You just quit the wild shots, that's all. Isn't it?"

"Yeah," Terry said. He paused again. "Well, it seems that there is more to the problem than that."

His father waited, watching Terry.

"The other guys have quit passing to me. They all figure that I'll just take a wild shot if I get the ball. The whole thing has hurt the team."

"Well, Terry. . . ." His father seemed flabbergasted.

Terry looked at his father. There was no use trying to hide anything. He took a deep breath. "I was trying to score all the goals myself," he said. "I was trying to be the star."

"You were hot dogging—"

"Bones Nelson called it showboating." Terry found the word easier to say than he had expected.

"—and you got benched for it," his father continued.

"That's about it."

"You'll have a chance to play some, though, won't you? I mean, you're not off the team, are you?"

"Coach Schmidt said that I still would get some playing time."

"Then you'll have a chance to win your way back onto the starting lineup—if you play the game the right way."

Terry did not feel like smiling. But he mustered a small smile. "That's what Coach Schmidt said. I can win my way back."

Sharp whistles brought the warm-up drills to a finish. The players ran toward the bench, gathering around Schmidt for the last words of advice and the announcement of the starting lineup.

In the bleachers, all the fans were in their seats awaiting the opening play.

Above the west bleachers, in the press box, Owen Milliman had his copy of the starting lineup now, ready to read it on the public-address system as the players took the field. Terry looked up at the press box. His friend would be surprised at the change at left forward. Terry glanced at the crowd in the bleachers. His father and mother were in there somewhere. But no one else in the crowd knew that Terry Masters was about to be benched. Terry wondered if any of the football players were in the crowd. Probably so. He could hear their exclamations now: "Hey, did you get that? Masters isn't on the starting lineup. How about that?"

At the outer edge of the circle of players, a referee moved around the players, bent low, making the routine inspection of cleats. The players unconsciously lifted one foot when the referee's striped shirt came into the edge of their peripheral vision. Then when the referee said, "Okay," they dropped the foot to the ground and lifted the other foot.

Terry was standing on one foot, the referee behind him, when Horst Schmidt reached the end of the starting lineup.

". . . at left forward, Butch Sterling."

The referee said, "Okay."

The word echoed through the suddenly silent circle of players around the coach. Then the elated Butch Sterling repeated it: "Oh-kaaay!"

Terry lifted his other foot for the referee.

In the instant before the starters turned to take the field for the beginning of the match, Terry's eyes met Bones's in a straight gaze, and then Wiz's. They both were surprised. That was obvious. Terry was relieved that he had known in advance and that they had not. Bones, it seemed, almost smiled. His eyes showed it. Wiz looked embarrassed. A hand touched Terry's shoulder from behind, and he turned. Hank Dodsworth said, "It'll work out."

The starters raced onto the field to take up their positions. Owen Milliman was reading the starting lineups on the public-address system. Terry backed up and sat down on the bench.

For the first time in his life, in any sport, Terry Masters was going to watch the start of an athletic contest from the bench.

Chapter 20

By half time the Eagles were trailing the Broncos by a 2–1 score.

Terry, heading for the dressing room with the other players, glanced at the scoreboard: Eagles 1, Visitors 2. It was the first time in the Eagles' thirteen matches to date that they had trailed an opponent.

Behind the retreating players, on the cinder track alongside the field, the Windsor High cheerleaders tried to coax some enthusiasm out of the stunned crowd. They had little luck. The fans had come to see their undefeated

Eagles march over the Hillcrest Broncos, an average team carrying a 7–5 won-lost record into the match.

But the Broncos seemed unable to do any wrong. They dominated the first half even more than the scoreboard indicated.

True enough, the loss of Henrik Sterner at sweeper was hurting the Eagles. Equally true, Terry told himself, the benching of Terry Masters until the last five minutes of the first half was hurting the Eagles. But also hurting the Eagles was a Hillcrest Broncos team that was fired up to play its best match of the season. The Broncos deserved their 2–1 lead at the intermission.

Until Terry took the field in the waning minutes of the first half, he sat slouched back on the bench, staring somberly at the action in front of him. First, his thoughts had been on Butch Sterling. Would Butch, given this chance, play well? Would he play well enough, perhaps, to keep Terry Masters on the bench?

The Broncos jumped to a 1–0 lead on a header out of a crowd in front of the goal, a short shot that Hank Dodsworth had neither the chance of anticipating nor the time to stop. Terry figured the Broncos owed that one to Henrik Sterner's broken ankle. They never would have succeeded in getting the ball so close to the goal if Henrik, instead of Jimmy Robinson, had been patrolling the area.

A few minutes later Butch, trying to pass, lost the ball to the challenge of a Hillcrest player in a brief but fierce duel. Terry glanced at Horst Schmidt, standing to his left at the sideline. Perhaps Horst Schmidt knew that he had erred in benching Terry. Perhaps he knew now that the Eagles needed Terry Masters on the field. But Schmidt showed nothing. He stood at the sideline, frowning at the field, exactly as he had done in each of the Eagles' twelve victorious matches, occasionally shouting "Close it up, close it up," or "Keep moving, keep moving." Nothing had changed with the coach. Nothing, that is, except that Horst Schmidt's Eagles were losing the match. Terry concentrated on Butch Sterling again.

But while Terry watched the racing figures on the field, an uncomfortable thought entered his mind. It was no more than a flicker at first, mildly unsettling. Then, with every turn in the play on the field, the thought grew. It remained even when the Eagles, on a sensational twenty-footer by Wiz, tied the score at 1–1. It was still there when the Broncos came right back to recapture the lead on a bit of fancy dribbling and a perfect pass followed by a perfect shot on goal from in close.

By the time Terry ran onto the field to replace Butch Sterling with five minutes remaining in the half, he was completely convinced: The Eagles were missing the play of Henrik Sterner at sweeper more than the play of Terry Masters, even at his best, at left forward. The Eagles were losing the match, not because Terry Masters was on the bench, not even because Terry Masters *and* Henrik Sterner

189

were missing from the field, but because Henrik was out. The big gap was at sweeper.

The thought was not a pleasant one for Terry. He was used to being needed when he was out. However, the fact was that Butch Sterling had played well in his place. Not as well as Terry at his best, Terry told himself, but well enough. In contrast, there was no replacement for Henrik. Nobody covered the defensive half of the field like Henrik. Jimmy Robinson was trying, to be sure, but Jimmy had neither the skills, the instincts, nor the power that Henrik brought to the task.

On the field in the thick of the play at last, Terry realized even more how much the loss of Henrik was hurting the Eagles. The impact of his absence was felt all the way to the forward line in front of the Broncos' goal.

Wiz, at center halfback, was playing his poorest match of the season. It was not Wiz's fault. He simply missed the surefooted feeds and the strong defensive backup from Henrik. Wiz, keeping one eye on the Eagles' weakened defense, was tending to keep back. His help was needed when the Broncos sent a long kick sailing deep into the Eagles' territory. Normally, with Henrik behind him, Wiz was quick to charge forward to add to the attack. But without Henrik, Wiz was late in adding his strength to the Eagles' drive for the goal, if he made it at all.

Terry, at forward, felt the added pressure of doing without Wiz, all because Henrik Sterner was missing from the field.

Now, walking across the end of the field toward the dressing room, Terry could not help asking himself if his absence, like Henrik's, was felt by his teammates from one end of the field to the other. The clear answer was no.

"Coach," Terry called out, as the players began forming into single file to enter the door to the gymnasium and the corridor to the dressing room.

Horst Schmidt, making his way toward the door with the players, turned. He frowned. "Yes, what?"

Terry stepped back away from the line of players, hoping the coach would join him.

Schmidt stepped out of the line, but only slightly. He said, "The intermission is not long. We have a lot of work. What is it that you want?" His voice carried a note of irritation.

Terry knew the thought that was in the coach's mind. Horst Schmidt was expecting Terry to issue one more plea, based on the bad news on the scoreboard. Horst Schmidt figured that Terry was assuming the Eagles were trailing because he—Terry Masters—was not playing. The coach's thoughts were clearly evident in his annoyed expression. Terry flushed slightly, embarrassed at what he was reading in Horst Schmidt's mind.

"I've got an idea," Terry said.

Coach Schmidt took another step toward Terry. The last of the players were filing through the door into the gymnasium. "A what?" Schmidt asked.

"An idea," Terry repeated.

Schmidt turned his head and watched the last player disappear through the door. "All right," he said, turning back to Terry, "but be quick about it."

The players had toweled off the sweat, taken their drinks of water, and were seated on the benches in front of the lockers. There was no chatter. The room was silent. The undefeated Windsor High Eagles were losing. Worse yet, it was no fluke. The Hillcrest Broncos were outplaying them every step of the way. The Hillcrest Broncos were going to come out the winners of the match, for sure, unless the Eagles came up with a way to turn the tide.

"Everyone here?" Schmidt asked, looking at the faces around him, seeming to be taking a mental count. "Nobody in there?" he asked, gesturing toward the side room with the toilets.

Bones Nelson, from the end of the bench where he could see, said, "Nobody in there."

"Okay," Schmidt said. He took a moment to glance at the players, one by one. "Okay, we are going to make some changes in the second half."

Terry held his breath. He had no inkling of what was coming. Horst Schmidt had listened to Terry's idea, standing outside the gymnasium door. He had not rejected it, but he had not said that he bought it either.

"Let me play sweeper," Terry had blurted.

Schmidt had stared at Terry without speaking. In the

moment of quiet, Terry got the strong impression that the coach had had the same idea himself. Something in Horst Schmidt's eyes said so. But Schmidt said nothing.

"I can do it," Terry said. "I'm stronger than Jimmy, and quicker. I've got the game experience, and Jimmy doesn't. Butch is doing a good job at forward. He can play there. What we need is a strong sweeper. I know I can do it."

"Do you really?" Schmidt spoke the words evenly. There was no trace of sarcasm. There was no bite to the question. It was a simple inquiry.

Terry began to speak quickly, the words rushing out. "I want to play—I can play—the team needs me—needs me at sweeper. At sweeper there's no problem of Bones and Wiz and Archie passing to me. At sweeper I'll be passing to them—so they can score—you said yourself, that was the big problem—their impression of me. What's their impression got to do with it if I'm at sweeper? I can do it." Terry stopped, breathless.

Schmidt watched Terry for a moment. Then he said, "We've got to get ourselves inside."

Now the coach was talking about the second half. "Krystian, you are delaying too long in moving forward on the attack. You are needed up there to add to our pressure on their defense when we are going to the goal. Terry will start the second half at sweeper." Coach Schmidt nodded slightly at Jimmy Robinson. While addressing Wiz, he seemed to be speaking for Jimmy's benefit. "It is to give you a player with some game experience backing you up in the defense. And you, Bones"—he shifted his gaze around the room to the little center forward—"I want you to. . . ."

Terry, leaning forward on a bench, hands clasped between his legs, sighed. There it was, the statement from the coach dropped into the middle of his half-time talk as if it were nothing. But it was everything. Terry consciously kept his face expressionless. He looked from the coach to the floor. He did not want to meet the eyes of any of his teammates.

Chapter 21

When Terry took the field for the start of the second half, he felt, well, backwards. Instead of cutting to his left, taking up a forward position and eyeing the opponent's goalie, he turned to his right. This time he headed for the end of the field where Hank Dodsworth stood in the penalty area in his familiar goalie sweatshirt of red and white stripes.

"We'll kill 'em," Hank shouted to Terry.

Terry waved in acknowledgment without turning. He was concentrating on the strangely reversed field of play that lay before him. He had never, even in the park-district league, played sweeper or even fullback. He always had been a forward, up front where the scoring was done. He never had played a defensive position. The thought occurred to him that he had always been in a scoring role in every sport.

In front of Terry the fullbacks were spread across the field. Chuck Horton, at his center fullback position, gestured for Terry to move forward. So he jogged up to a position just behind and to the right of Chuck.

The right fullback, Woody Clark, turned and grinned at Terry. "Hey, welcome to the world of defense," he called out.

Terry nodded. He was watching Wiz at the center spot. The scene was strange from this angle. Wiz was half turned, facing away from Terry, awaiting the referee's signal to begin play. The Eagles were going to dribble or pass the ball toward the other end of the field—not toward Terry, but away from him. The position felt strange.

In the moment before the match resumed, Terry felt his first doubts. Suddenly he was troubled. Never had Terry doubted his ability to play any game. Typically, he felt no doubt when the idea of playing sweeper first jelled in his mind. He had not questioned his ability to play sweeper when he made the suggestion to Horst Schmidt. He was fast and quick on the soccer field. He could kick with strength and accuracy. And, after all, defense was defense, wasn't it? On a soccer field, everybody played some defense. So what was there to doubt? In the dressing room, when Horst Schmidt announced that Terry was starting at sweeper in the second half, Terry had felt only relief and excitement.

When he was getting to his feet to leave the dressing room, and his eyes met Bones's and Wiz's briefly, Terry saw no doubts in their eyes, either. He saw only surprise and confusion. Schmidt had not said that the idea came from Terry. Had Terry Masters, the glory hog, even known that the coach was going to insert him at the sweeper position? What did Terry think of it? How was Terry going to like chasing after fancy-footed dribblers instead of being one? Could the showboater take it? Those were the questions written in their puzzled stares. For Terry, their puzzlement provided a sense of satisfaction. Let them wonder! There was no room in his mind then for doubts about his ability to play the sweeper position.

When he was standing at the sideline and he heard the raspy voice of Owen Milliman announcing to the crowd, "A change in the Eagles' lineup, Terry Masters at sweeper," and the murmur of the crowd, Terry was pleased. He knew that his father would read the meaning of the announcement correctly: Terry was winning his way back. Terry wondered what the football players in the crowd must be saying now. He had imagined their remarks at the news he was being benched. Now he imagined their confusion. He was at a new position, to be sure, but he was starting the second half. He had no doubts at all.

Now, however, watching Wiz pass the ball off to Jorge, who dribbled toward the center, angling around the edge of the center circle, Terry felt horribly out of position. He did not know whether to edge forward with the flow of the play or hold his ground. His soccer instincts told him nothing. Finally he stepped forward, between and slightly behind Chuck and Woody, following the movement of the ball under Jorge's steady control.

Terry wracked his brain for the bits of coaching advice he had heard—heard only absently—Horst Schmidt hammering at Henrik Sterner since the season began: Avoid being caught between the touchline and your opponent. . . . Keep the player with the ball to the outside, and let him dribble all the way to the goal line if he wants. . . . If your goalie has to come out onto the field to deal with a high center, fall back to help protect the goal. . . . If you intercept a pass, your best setup for our attack is a short, accurate pass—maybe a push pass—to a winger. . . . Any kick removing the ball from the penalty area is a good kick. . . . Help out others in the defense, but don't leave any of the attackers in your area too free to move around. . . . Always crowd a dribbler, but not so closely that he can sprint away from you. . . . What else? What else?

Up front, Jorge, in trouble, dropped the ball off to Wiz.

Wiz quickly passed over to Paul Chandler. Paul, the weakest of the Eagles' halfbacks, took in the pass uncertainly, then hesitated. Two Bronco defenders converged on him. The ball squirted free. A Hillcrest fullback laid his foot into the free ball and sent it sailing over the halfway line down the touchline. A Hillcrest winger outjumped Woody Clark and headed the ball on an angle down the field and toward the center.

Terry raced over behind Chuck Horton, who was scampering toward the ball. Chuck's knee caught a piece of the bounding ball but nothing more. His off-center kick sent the ball trickling weakly to the right, where it bounced off a surprised Bronco player and disappeared into a tangle of thrashing feet and legs.

Terry advanced toward the crowd. The situation was dangerous. The confusion was occurring just outside the penalty area in front of the Eagles' goal. A solid kick out of the crowd by a Bronco could spell goal. Even a wild kick—with luck—could score. Anybody's kick, from a Bronco or an Eagle, could set up the ball for a header in front of the Eagles' goal. Terry glanced back. Hank was dancing in the goal mouth, concentrating on the swirling action in front of him. Ahead of Terry, the ball suddenly spurted out to the side. Terry charged forward. He caught the ball on his thigh. As the ball, under Terry's control, dropped to the ground, a Bronco appeared suddenly from Terry's left. Terry booted the ball gently to a clear area to the side and raced after it, against the grain of the advancing Bronco player's path. The Bronco player swerved, but too late. He lost a step on Terry. The loss was fatal. Beating the pursuing Bronco to the ball, Terry kicked a low line drive to Paul Chandler near the sideline, just beyond the halfway line.

The crowd in the bleachers roared approval of the save.

Behind him, Terry heard Hank's shout, "Way to go!"

Terry grinned. He had won his first encounter as a sweeper.

Upfield, Paul took in the pass on his chest and dropped the ball off to Wiz, who had come racing over to back him up. Wiz fired a pass to Bones in front of the goal. The Broncos, caught out of position by the rapid-fire combination of two lengthy passes, both perfect, were outnumbered in front of the goal. Bones took in the pass on his instep. He paused a second, the ball on the ground under his foot. Then he turned, dribbled briefly to elude a defender, and faked a shot on goal. The Broncos' goalie took the bait. He lunged to his left. Bones sent a push pass to Butch Sterling on the opposite side. Butch, with half the goal mouth open before him, drilled the ball into the nets.

The score was tied 2–2. The Windsor crowd was on its feet cheering.

Up front, Butch danced gleefully toward Bones. Butch's first varsity goal of his career now was in the record books. Bones clasped him in a bear hug.

200

Terry, hearing the cheers, watched the scene. The goal was Butch's. The assist belonged to Bones. But Terry, almost up to the halfway line now, felt a glow of satisfaction. Terry's quick pickup of the loose ball, dangerously close to the Eagles' own goal, had started the scoring play. His pass to Paul had launched the successful attack.

"I didn't get the goal and I didn't get the assist," Terry told himself, "but I did assist the assist that assisted the assist that got the goal."

Terry was grinning at the thought when the Broncos' goalie sent the ball soaring toward midfield to resume the play. His doubts, so troublesome just a few moments ago, were gone.

"Back up, back up," Chuck was shouting at Terry.

Terry turned and raced to the rear, belatedly trying to take up his position.

The goalie's high kick came down in a crowd just short of the center circle. A taller Bronco outjumped Wiz for a header that sent the ball rocketing down the middle of the field toward the Eagles' goal. Out of nowhere, Chuck Horton materialized, stopping the ball with a thigh. Jorge Perez, following Chuck toward the action, raced toward the ball, picked it up smoothly in a dribble, and headed back toward midfield. Jorge, although overweight and slow, was a surefooted dribbler. In a zigzag pattern, he worked his way almost to the halfway line, then passed off to Wiz. The threat was ended.

For what seemed to Terry like an interminable period,

the two teams battled for the ball around the halfway line. First the Eagles had possession and lost it. Then the Broncos lost possession. Neither team was able to muster a serious scoring threat out of the fierce sequence of give-and-take at midfield.

Terry, increasingly grateful for Chuck Horton's good guidance—shouts and waves—hung back in his position, the last line of defense before Hank Dodsworth in the goal mouth.

Only once in the long series of exchanges did Terry handle the ball. A Bronco winger, dribbling down the touchline, turned Woody Clark around with a deft fake. Terry, running across to back Woody up, did not take the fake. He met the winger head on, sliding in for a perfect tackle, nicking the ball without touching the Bronco. The winger, his mind still on Woody, was taken by surprise. Woody zeroed in on the loose ball. As Terry was bouncing back to his feet, he saw Woody send a high, lofting kick back beyond the halfway line.

At the end of the third quarter, the scoreboard still showed: Eagles 2, Visitors 2.

Chapter 22

"Great going," Hank Dodsworth told Terry with a slap on the back, as they jogged to the sideline for the intermission.

"So far, so good," Terry replied. He was relieved that the Broncos were the opponents in this first effort at playing sweeper. The Broncos, far from the toughest team on the Eagles' schedule, were unable to take full advantage of the newcomer at sweeper for the Eagles. The two Mexican halfbacks of the Linden Tigers, Terry reflected, would have tied him in knots. They would have converted Terry's uncertainties into goals for themselves. "So far, so good," Terry repeated.

In the huddle around the coach at the bench, encouraging words came at Terry from every direction. "You're doing fine," Chuck Horton said.

"Just keep waving at me," Terry said with a smile.

Wiz moved up to Terry. "Nice playing," he said.

Bones Nelson chimed in, "Good going," he said.

To Terry's surprise, even Horst Schmidt, who was not given to passing out compliments in the midst of a match, told Terry, "You are playing well. Keep it up."

Terry blinked. "Thanks," he said.

Then the coach added, "That was a nice tackle you made on the player who faked Woody out of position, but don't do it again!"

Terry's smile faded. "Huh?" he said.

"If he had got past you, where would you have been? On the ground, that's where, and out of the play. Keep your feet. Stick with your man."

Terry nodded. He thought back to the startled expression on the Bronco's face when Terry went sliding into him feet first. The Bronco had been surprised, but perhaps not by Terry's sudden appearance so much as the tactic of the reckless tackle.

Schmidt moved quickly into the business of preparing his team for the fourth quarter. He cautioned Wiz about getting into leaping duels with the taller Bronco center half-back. "But if you must jump, do jump," he said. "Always challenge. Never let an opponent have the ball unchallenged. Always challenge." He asked Jorge how he felt.

The fourth quarter always found Jorge leg weary and winded. "I'm okay," Jorge said.

. Next Coach Schmidt turned to Bones and the other two forwards, pointing out that the Broncos' goalie had shown himself to be vulnerable to a fake. "He jumps in the direction of the first move every time. He's nervous. Keep him that way. Always give him a fake and shoot away from him, or pass quickly to the other side."

Finally Schmidt told Chuck Horton, with a glance at Terry, to move farther out toward midfield to meet the Broncos' advances. "We had Krystian hanging back too much in the first half, and now we've got you hanging back too much," he said. "Move out and let the sweeper do his job behind you."

Terry listened, and he knew that in the fourth quarter he was going to have to shoulder a greater share of the defense. His apprenticeship, a short one, was over. The score was tied. If the Eagles were to win, every player on the field—including the new sweeper—had to play errorless ball. True, the Hillcrest Broncos were not the measure of the Linden Tigers, but Terry reminded himself that they had jumped to a 2–1 half-time lead over the Eagles.

Taking the field to start the fourth quarter, Terry glanced at the Broncos' bench. The Broncos' coach was still talking as the players were walking onto the field. His voice was low, too low for Terry to hear what he was saying, but he was waving his hands excitedly. The last two players listening to him, both halfbacks, were nodding.

Remembering Horst Schmidt's advice to Chuck Horton, to move out and let the sweeper do his job, Terry could imagine the Hillcrest coach's instruction to his halfbacks: If the Eagles' fullbacks hang back to protect the new player at sweeper, charge ahead; you've got the midfield area. If the fullbacks move out against you, the new player at sweeper is left alone and is vulnerable; center the ball deep and go after him.

Almost immediately after the start of play, Terry felt the absence of Chuck and his partners at fullback, Woody Clark and Bob Traynor. They were playing only a yard or so farther upfield, but to Terry the distance seemed a mile. They were quicker to advance to meet the ball, widening the gap left for Terry. At first, Terry tended to edge forward with them. Several times he went too far. Chuck waved him back. Then Terry noticed the large expanse of field behind him. He must not leave it unguarded against the long pass or the sudden spurt of a dribbler coming out of a crowd with the ball.

With each assault of the Broncos, Terry raced toward the area of the ball. But he took care each time to keep himself in a position of support behind the fullbacks. Even when challenging a Bronco for the ball, he kept himself ready to turn and run toward the penalty area. Hank, lured out to stop a dangerously deep drive, would need help from the sweeper guarding the goal mouth. Terry launched into no more sliding tackles. Instead, he concentrated on driving dribblers to the sideline and keeping them on the outside.

Time and again the Eagles' outstanding defensive play—first the halfbacks at midfield, led by the quick-footed Wiz, and then the fullbacks behind them—stopped the Broncos. But the Broncos were stopping the Eagles too. Not once in the first ten minutes of the fourth quarter did either team get an open shot on goal. Both battered each other at midfield, struggling for control, probing for an opening that never came.

A Broncos' thrust halted at the halfway line when Paul Chandler, scampering alongside a dribbler, forced the Bronco player to tap the ball out-of-bounds. Paul stepped over the sideline, took the ball from the referee, and, with a strong overhead throw, sent it sailing into an open space in front of Wiz.

Wiz dashed after the ball, stopping it on the bounce with his left foot. He turned, edging the ball gently out of the way of an onrushing Bronco fullback. Then he pushed the ball back off to Paul, who was coming across in a deep arc.

Terry, moving up, held his breath as he watched the developing play. The stage was set for a goal. The Broncos' center fullback had moved far out to help a halfback intercept Wiz in the open space. The fullback's momentum carried him several steps farther in the wrong direction, past Wiz. The ball was going the other way, in the direction of the goal, toward Paul. The Broncos' left fullback was marking Paul, now racing toward the center. Between them the two fullbacks had left a giant void in the Broncos' defense. Beyond the action, the Broncos' nervous goalie, left almost

207

without help for the moment, shifted from one foot to the other, watching the movement of the ball.

Paul, with the Bronco defender in hot pursuit, took in Wiz's soft pass without breaking stride. Not the best receiver on the team and a shaky dribbler, Paul got the job done this time. A shoulder fake failed to shake off the Bronco marking him. So Paul screeched to a halt and turned quickly, his back to the goal. The Bronco, surprised, raced on past Paul. Paul turned again and kicked to his right, sending a ground pass to Archie McAlister in the hole left by the fullback. Archie brought the ball in.

Archie was alone and had time to shoot. But he took too much time. The Broncos' goalie raced over to face him. When Archie's left foot smacked the ball and sent it sailing toward the nets, the Broncos' goalie was there waiting. He caught the line drive easily.

Terry sighed as he backpedaled into position for the goalie's kick returning the ball to play. A quicker shot by Archie would have scored. Or, better yet, a fake to hold the goalie at the side, followed by a quick pass to Bones in the center, would have scored. Bones, with a clear line to the goal, seldom missed. Terry shrugged off the thought that he with the ball in that position would have scored for the Eagles.

Terry was still moving backward when the goalie's kick, veering to Terry's right, came down near the halfway line. Paul and a Bronco halfback battled for the ball, and the ball squirted away from the two of them into the center of the field.

From there, suddenly, the ball was coming at Terry, a low bullet of a kick flanked by the blurred forms of two Broncos in their orange shirts with black trim. Where had they all—the ball and the players—come from so quickly?

Terry heard a shout from Hank behind him. By this time he was driving with all his strength for the ball.

Terry reached the ball, now a line drive dropping to the ground. He planted his right foot, swung his left foot, and hit the ball squarely. The kick felt good. It was solid and on the mark.

But the ball traveled barely five yards. One of the blurred figures wearing the Bronco colors was in the path. The ball caromed off the knee of the startled Bronco. Another Bronco trapped the ball. Terry charged in to challenge him. He heard another shout from Hank behind him, but he did not understand the words.

Then, just as suddenly as the ball had first appeared, it disappeared. Terry was trying to duel with a Bronco who did not have the ball. He whirled, trying to see every place at the same time. Where had the ball gone? Behind him, Terry spotted the Bronco whose knee had deflected Terry's pass. He had the ball. The first Bronco had dropped it off to him immediately upon recovering the loose ball. Terry, in his quick charge, had been outsmarted. He had committed himself too quickly—and too completely. His opponent, seeing him coming, had passed off to a teammate. Terry had challenged nothing but air. He felt like a fool. A forward could survive a defensive error like that. After all, the forward had almost one hundred yards of playing field between himself and his team's goal at the other end. But the same error, committed by a sweeper in the shadow of his own goal, could be fatal.

The Bronco with the ball took aim. In the horror of the moment, Terry wondered where Hank was standing. Near the center, where Terry had thought the shot would come from? Or at the right side, where the Bronco was shooting? Or somewhere in between, trying to correct himself? Terry lunged at an imaginary line between kicker and goal. Perhaps he could block the kick again. But there was no contest. The Bronco did not make Paul Chandler's mistake. He did not take too much time and wait for Terry to recover. The kick, like a rifle shot, passed in front of Terry's frantic leap, heading for the goal.

Terry, falling in his forward plunge, turned in time to see Hank—horizontal in his desperate leap—spear the ball and hang on with his outstretched hands to save the goal.

Chuck Horton, coming in fast, helped Hank to his feet and wrapped his arms around the goalie in a giant bear hug of congratulations.

When Terry and Hank looked at each other, Terry puffed his cheeks and blew out a stream of air in a silent exclamation: Whew! Hank was grinning.

210

Jorge Perez got Hank's kick resuming the play. He moved down the sideline skillfully. Trapped finally, he passed around the Bronco marking him to the waiting Butch Sterling. Butch pushed the ball back out toward the center into an open spot, and Wiz was there when the ball arrived. The Eagles were moving the ball almost at will. Wiz, tackled by the Bronco marking him, managed to get the ball off with a weak pass back to Butch. Butch, surrounded and harassed, retreated to a point near the goal line, off to the side.

Terry, with the ball so deep in the other end of the field, was standing almost at the halfway line, watching. He lost sight of the ball in the scrambling crowd that surrounded Butch. Then he saw the referee signal out-of-bounds, over the goal line, last touched by a Bronco. The play set up a corner kick for the Eagles. Wiz moved over to position himself for the kick. The Eagles' forwards ganged up in front of the goal.

"Terry!"

Terry turned toward the sound and looked at Horst Schmidt at the sideline.

The coach was waving his right arm in a large circle, gesturing Terry toward the Broncos' goal.

Puzzled, Terry pointed a finger at his own chest.

"Yes, you!" Schmidt shouted. "Corner kick. Take it!"

Terry broke into a run. He was surprised. The Eagles didn't usually bring the sweeper up for a corner kick. He

211

covered the fifty yards to the crowd in front of the Broncos' goal just before Wiz stepped into the ball. Wiz sent a perfect kick, soft and hovering, into the penalty area.

Terry, watching the ball, timed himself and went up for a header shot on goal. He turned, head up, keeping his eyes on the ball. At the last second he snapped his body, then his head, forward. His forehead popped against the ball. He knew he had the goal. He could feel it. The contact was perfect.

But he didn't. The ball, going a shade too high, hit the crossbar and bounced straight back over the crowd of players, landing at the edge of the penalty arc.

Terry, realizing what had happened, thrashed his way out of the crowd of players and headed for the loose ball. Then he stopped. With the ball free and in play, should he head back for his defensive position? Or should he go for the ball? In the instant of his doubt, Jorge Perez swept over from the left and picked off the ball. Jorge passed quickly to Bones, who was moving now through the right side of the penalty area. Bones had an open alley to the goal. The goalie was out of position by a half step, having concentrated on Jorge on the other side. Bones pumped the ball into the goal.

The scoreboard blinked: Eagles 3, Visitors 2. A roaring cheer rolled down from the bleachers.

Bones, holding both hands in the air, skipped and ran toward Paul Chandler, the nearest player. Paul met him with a shout and a hug.

Terry, heading back to his sweeper position, patted Bones on the shoulder. "Beauty, beauty," he said.

Bones, clearly surprised, gave Terry a startled look.

Terry shrugged and raced downfield to take up the defense.

Chapter 23

The final four minutes were wild. The Eagles had to with-
stand a series of frantic Bronco attacks aimed at tieing and
then winning the match. Time and again the Broncos' long
kicks penetrated deep into the Eagles' territory. At the end
of each of them, the fullbacks, along with Terry from his
sweeper position, collided in fierce skirmishes with the
determined Broncos. The Broncos had smelled a great upset
over the Eagles. Now they were seeing their chances slip
out of their grasp. They flailed wildly, centering the ball
at every opportunity and charging into the melee, hoping

214

against hope that somebody's foot or head or knee would send the ball into the Eagles' goal.

But the Eagles' fullbacks, with Terry scrambling in their midst and Hank Dodsworth guarding the goal mouth, held the Broncos off every time, and finally the clock ran out.

At the finish Terry stood on the field, motionless for a moment, breathing heavily. The closing minutes of the match had been the most torturous time he could remember on an athletic field. The extreme physical exertion—the constant running to challenge, to intercept, to tackle—was nothing new to Terry. The unrelenting pressure of a desperate opponent was not new. But the unfamiliar position at a different end of the field *was* new. The unsureness, the uncomfortable sort of tentativeness, the lack of confidence in his own instincts were new ingredients in athletic combat for Terry Masters, and he felt their burden.

The onslaught finally had ended. The clock finally had run down. The match finally reached its finish. And the scoreboard lights recorded the score:

Eagles 3, Broncos 2.

The atmosphere in the Eagles' dressing room was more one of weary relief than of triumphant exhilaration.

Terry, seated on a bench, silently took a moment of rest before pulling off his uniform and going to the showers. Beside him, Hank peeled off his red-and-white striped goalie's shirt, tossed it in the locker, draped a towel over his shoulders, and turned to Terry.

"You're going to stay at sweeper, aren't you?" he asked. "I mean, you're not going back to forward, are you?"

Terry glanced up at his friend. Without answering, he turned and looked across the dressing room. Horst Schmidt, standing near the training table, was eyeing him. Terry knew the same questions were going through the coach's mind. Would the football runner, the basketball scorer, the baseball cleanup hitter settle for an unglamorous defensive role in soccer? Maybe Schmidt had heard Hank's question. The dressing room was quiet. There was no cheering, no shouting, no joking in the wake of the narrow victory. Hank's words, though softly spoken, might have carried to the coach's ears.

Terry turned back to Hank. "I don't know," he said. Then he got to his feet, took a deep breath, and walked across the dressing room to the coach.

Behind him, the dressing room was silent. Someone, Terry did not know who, was already in the showers around the corner. But most of the players were still in the dressing room, toweling off the perspiration and slowly removing their game uniforms. Terry was sure he could feel the gaze of a dozen sets of eyes on the back of his head.

"You played well," Schmidt said, as Terry approached.

The compliment caught Terry by surprise. Horst Schmidt

216

seldom delivered individual praise, especially in a quiet dressing room full of players listening to every word. But the compliment came as even more of a surprise because he knew—for the first time in his athletic career—that he had not played well. He had made mistakes. He had committed tactical errors. He had overshot attackers in his zeal to stop them. He had, because of his inexperience, floundered out of position, needing Woody or Chuck or Bob to bail him out. He remembered Hank's spectacular save after Terry had failed to block a Bronco's kick on goal.

"I. . . ."

"Eh?" Schmidt prompted.

Behind him, Terry heard a bench scrape on the concrete floor. He heard the voice of someone walking into the showers. Somebody else answered. Maybe, after all, everyone in the dressing room was not watching, not listening. Perhaps they could not hear him.

"I hope I can stay at sweeper," Terry said finally. "I think that's the place for me. I can learn. I'll get better. I—"

"Yes," said Schmidt, "Yes." He smiled slightly, seeming unsurprised by Terry's statement. "Yes," he repeated. "I think that is what we should do."

Terry blinked at the coach. He decided to finish what he had started to say. "That's where the team needs me," he said.

"Yes."

Terry waited a moment, then nodded and turned and walked back to the locker.

"Well?" Hank asked.

"Huh?"

"What was that all about?"

Before Terry could reply, the dressing-room door flew open and Henrik Sterner came hobbling in on crutches, a white cast protruding from his slashed trouser leg.

"What's this I hear about you winning without me?" he called out to the room in general. His face wore an expression of exaggerated astonishment. "It can't be true," he said.

Somehow the spectacle of Henrik brought home to the players the fact that, yes, they had won, and a ripple of laughter broke the quiet of the dressing room.

Alongside Terry, Hank piped up, "Weren't you out there on the field? I didn't notice."

There was more laughter as Henrik glared at Hank in mock anger. "There I was, in the emergency room, all pain and agony. But was I thinking about that? No, I was worrying about my teammates needing me. And what do you say now? Not only did you win without me,"—he snorted —"but—"

Horst Schmidt interrupted Henrik's monologue. "Can you teach Terry Masters to play sweeper?"

Bones Nelson, coming out of the shower with a towel around his waist, heard Schmidt's question and stopped in his tracks. He looked at Terry. Wiz, seated on a bench re-

218

moving his shoes, looked up at Terry. Hank, standing by Terry, was grinning.

Terry, with all eyes on him, watched Henrik.

"You?" Henrik said.

Terry nodded.

"You played sweeper tonight?"

Terry shrugged. "Well, sort of," he said with a grin.

"What do you know about playing sweeper?"

"Well, more now than I used to."

"It was Terry's idea," Schmidt said. "And he wants to stick with the job, now that you're sidelined with that." He pointed at the cast.

"And you guys won?" Henrik asked, doing a good job of sounding incredulous.

Schmidt lifted himself to a seat on the training table. He seemed to be enjoying the exchange. "Terry made some mistakes, but you can teach him," he said. "You can teach him."

"I don't know," Henrik said slowly, a deep frown creasing his forehead. "Terry always struck me as a slow learner."

Terry grinned. "I think I'll undress and go to the shower," he said, "just to get away from you."

Bones, standing in the door from the showers, was gaping at Terry.

Terry grinned at Bones. He could not help it. Bones had been surprised when he shouted his congratulations after the game-winning goal. Now Bones was flabbergasted.

Terry Masters, at his own suggestion, was going to play sweeper, far from the scorer's spotlight. He could not believe it. Terry enjoyed the sight of Bones's astonishment.

Terry pulled off his shirt. Then he turned and sat down on the bench to remove his shoes. He looked up to find Bones, still clutching the towel around his waist, standing in front of him.

"I think I owe you an apology," Bones said. He extended his right hand.

Everyone in the room was watching. Terry, feeling himself blush, took Bones's hand.

"No, I'm the one who owes the apology," Terry said. "You see, you were right—for a while."

They pumped hands solemnly in the awkward silence. Neither seemed to know what to say next. Neither wanted to be the first to release the grasp.

After a moment that seemed like an hour, Wiz broke the silence. "Terry, you have quite a record to live up to at the sweeper position," he said.

Terry and Bones released their grip.

"Yes, I know," Terry said. "Henrik—"

"Oh, I don't mean Henrik."

"Huh?"

"You were part of a shutout—that's the word, isn't it? —a shutout defense in the second half," Wiz said. "No points scored."

Terry remembered the mistakes—the failures, the poor

positioning, the missed interceptions—but he managed a grin. "Say, yeah, that's right, isn't it?"

Schmidt came off the training table. "When you heroes have finished congratulating yourselves," he said, "you'd better shower and dress before you take your death of cold."

About the Author

Thomas J. Dygard was born in Little Rock, Arkansas, and received a B.A. degree from the University of Arkansas, Fayetteville. He began his career as a sportswriter for the *Arkansas Gazette* in Little Rock and joined the Associated Press in 1954. Since then, he has worked in A.P. offices in Little Rock, Detroit, Birmingham, New Orleans, and Indianapolis. At present, he is Chief of Bureau in Chicago.

Mr. Dygard is married, has two children, and now lives in Arlington Heights, Illinois.